Saucy Sad Sexy *Sinister*

By J D Wilson

The Perfect Marriage

A Song for Lionel

She Married for Money

Son of the Ripper

The Café of Your Dreams

Freddy Fogg's Rebellion

The Clone Conspiracies

The Man Who Squashed the World

A Horse Called Harry

Assassin by Post

The Midwinter Murders

Lost in a Dream

1918

The Perfect Marriage

You can't go to jail for what you're thinking.....'

So goes the song, but it does not stop you feeling *guilty* for what you're thinking. It was being played on the radio and it triggered Muriel's secret thoughts.

Silly really as she was only *thinking*, and not even about another man. Well, not *really*. Not a *particular* man. It was just, oh Howard was a good husband. But oh, if only he was more like … and she stopped, because she not sure what she wanted Howard to be more like. All she knew was that he was so…so *boring!* There! She had said it.

Still she felt guilty because it was not Howard's fault, bless him. He worked hard as an accountant and pensions analyst and one day they will have paid for their apartment in a nice part of New York. Life with Howard was comfortable but oh, sometimes, she longed for something more than just *comfortable*.

They lived reasonably well, not really short of money. It had become a habit to watch their spending; nothing wild or extravagant. Sensible, of course, as their investments were designed to give them a comfortable retirement. There it was, that word again: comfortable!

One day money would be plentiful when all the endowments and investment portfolios Howard had set up came to fruition, but a rich old age was not what Muriel longed for.

What she wanted was a bit of WOW! in her life now, the sort of WOW! she reckoned the man she had passed that morning in the street could give a girl.

Tall and dark and just oozing money, Muriel fancied he had given her a look. Not just a look but a *look*. There is a difference. They had passed each other a lot lately, and Muriel was beginning to think it was not by accident.

No, not a *particular* man. She would not call him a particular man. But she was sure he had given her a look.

No, guilty thoughts again, and she focused on what to get for dinner.

Howard was thinking about dinner too. Muriel was a wonderful cook. He always enjoyed his meals, but thinking this made him feel oddly guilty. Why should he feel guilty? Muriel was a good wife, but thinking this made him feel even guiltier. Somehow he had no right to be enjoying the meals of someone he was feeling guilty about. What was wrong with him?

He felt different today, and could hardly concentrate on his work. Instead he found himself thinking about that woman. That was why he was feeling guilty. Why on earth should he feel guilty? He was only *thinking!*

The woman had entered the office the day before, tall and exotic and oozing sex appeal. She was one of Brett Bellamy's clients, lucky devil. Bellamy was a flash character and had winked at Howard as he ushered her into his office and whispered: "Not for old married men, eh Howard?"

Perhaps this is how midlife crises in men are triggered. Something happens that makes a man realise he is missing out on life, and time is passing him by. A chance remark; a chance meeting.

Still, he felt guilty. Muriel was a wonderful woman and a good wife. But, oh, she was so...so *boring*.

There! He had said it!

Speaking of boring, Muriel had been concerned lately about finding the newspapers difficult to read.

"I think I need glasses," she said at the dinner table one evening, which was about as boring a subject as she could think of, apart from Howard talking about pension funds.

Not that Howard, bless him, talked to her about pension funds at home, but he always did whenever they were at a social function. The social functions they usually attended always seemed to be full of men like Howard, accountants, pensions analysts and so on. It was what everybody wanted to talk to him about, which only emphasised to Muriel that being married to Howard was boring.

"Well, my dear, you must get yourself some," said Howard immediately.

"They will be expensive," said Muriel.

"Eyesight is very important," replied Howard. "Don't worry about the money!"

Dear sensible Howard, thought Muriel, such a thoughtful husband, and she sighed.

Howard sighed as well, as he had been thinking that he too ought to get some glasses as he found reading small print difficult these days. Sometimes in dull light he did not recognise acquaintances in the street until he had almost bumped into them. Glasses! A sign of what? Middle age on the horizon, that's what glasses were a sign of!

Muriel did not like the idea of glasses either, not at her age, and said no more. Howard knew that if he said anything about needing glasses Muriel, bless her, would fuss until he got some, so he said nothing.

Life plodded on.

Muriel took to walking slowly on her way to the supermarket hoping to see that tall dark man again. Then one day there he was, and her heartbeat quickened. There was a woman on his arm, expensively dressed and elegant; the sort of woman who always has a rich handsome escort and never cooked dinner every evening for a boring husband!

The man gave her a polite smile as he passed and Muriel realised that it had all been in her imagination. She stood no chance against a woman like that!

So her life might have continued in the same old way, but for a chance meeting in the café in Macy's, New York's plushest department store. Muriel liked to go there to dream.

This morning she got chatting to a rich woman as they were having coffee. 'Rich' is how Muriel had immediately categorised her as it was obvious from her clothes and her conversation that money was no object. The woman was in Macy's to add a few thousand dollars-worth of absolute essentials to her wardrobe.

When they had finished their coffee the woman surprised Muriel by saying: "I would love your opinion on an outfit I have been looking at." She persuaded Muriel to go with her to the fashion department where she tried it on.

Muriel enviously praised her in the outfit and then the woman said: "Why don't you try it on, they have your size."

Muriel, encouraged by the woman, put it on and received glowing praise. This was exciting, and soon she was trying more outfits. Muriel was enjoying herself, indulging her fantasy of looking like a million dollars.

"You've got a good figure," the woman told her. "Your clothes have been hiding it!" Looking at herself in the mirror Muriel was pleasantly surprised to see the woman was right.

Then it happened. At that very moment Howard, who was in the store to buy some office supplies, happened to walk by. On impulse the woman collared him for an opinion.

"Here's a gentleman. Tell me, what do you think of this lady in her new outfit?"

Then to Muriel's astonishment Howard peered at her, and nodded. "Delightful," he answered, and added with somewhat uncharacteristic sauciness (for Howard). "Someone's a lucky man!"

An embarrassed Muriel was about to scold him for being silly but he walked on and she realised that he really had not recognised her.

She watched him walk away, still expecting that any second that he would turn around and laugh, having tricked her. Then he did stop and looked back at her, and she could see that he meant what he had said - but still had no idea who she was.

Muriel went home that afternoon in a daze.

Now things were happening to Muriel. The mould in which she had been living was beginning to break up. She took to looking at herself in the mirror and wondering why she had to wear bargain store clothes. And there was no reason at all - except money!

It did not take long once that process was started for her to find a way to scrimp the money together from their weekly budget and start buying clothes to re-create that Macy Muriel.

That backward look from Howard in the fashion department - he had fancied her!

It was uncharacteristic of Howard, but he had been so taken by the sexy woman he had just met in Macy's when he got back to the office he told Brett Bellamy about her. Bellamy was amused by this, coming from staid old Howard, and joked: "Watch out Howard, you'll be having an affair if you aren't careful."

Howard was embarrassed but put on a smirk, macho-style.

"Do you good, Howard," Brett told him in his usual brash manner.

"What would?"

"Having an affair."

"Not me, couldn't do that to Muriel."

Brett loved to tease him. "Ah, but how do you know she doesn't have a toyboy secreted away somewhere, eh Howard?"

"Rubbish! Not my Muriel!"

As on every evening Muriel was in the kitchen when Howard arrived home. Same old Muriel. He greeted her with his customary peck on the cheek.

Muriel sighed. Same old Howard, but she was a brand new Muriel with a secret life!

But Howard was not the same old Howard. This Howard was the one who in Macy's had seen the sexiest woman he had seen in a long time.

Recalling his bold flirtatious comment 'lucky man!' that had jumped spontaneously from his lips, he felt pretty good. This Howard was even thinking that maybe Bellamy was right. Perhaps an affair did do a man good.

And now that Howard had been awakened, as it were, to things rather more interesting than accountancy, Bellamy's banter about an affair kept popping up. That led on to a startling thought - ridiculous of course - could Muriel be having an affair? There was something different about her these days…something - no, ridiculous!

Disappointing as the tall dark man had been, Muriel was not downhearted for long. This was the new Muriel, the Muriel of Macy's fashion department.

In her new outfits Muriel hardly recognised herself. They revealed her good figure to full advantage, which her sensibly-priced clothes had not flattered. Things were different now! So she took to slipping out dressed to the nines and walking in Central Park and enjoying the looks from passing men. She was feeling good about herself, and when women are dressed in their best and feeling their best, men look, my word how they *look!*

One day, chatting to a group of fashionable women in Macy's café, she was asked her name. It must have been destiny, because the name of a Hollywood actress Zara Storm whom Muriel admired just popped into her mind.

"Zara," she answered, and realising that Zara Storm would hardly ring true, trawled hastily through all the weather words she could think of and came up with rainbow.

"Zara Bow."

"Zara! What a lovely name," they all agreed, and Muriel - no, Zara! - felt welcomed into their company as a worthy fashionista.

Muriel saw a picture of Zara Storm wearing some very stylish glasses and she got herself a pair just like them. They made her feel even sexier, and as a bonus she could see better.

Thereafter whenever she dressed up, she fell automatically into being Zara Bow. It was the persona she was meant to be!

Fortunately there was a large cupboard in the corridor attached to every flat, which they never used, and Muriel was able to slip into it to change from Muriel to Zara and vice versa. That way there was no danger of her arriving at their flat and bumping into Howard dressed as Zara!

Meeting that dishy woman in Macy's fashion department had followed another incident in the office that was changing Howard's outlook on life. He overheard the office girls discussing the men they worked with. They were compiling a list of the sexiest and he, Howard, came bottom, accompanied by giggles.

So, with all that, and seeing that gorgeous woman, Howard decided. He was going to smarten himself up. With a new purpose in his step he left the office and headed for 59th and Bloomingdale's, where he had heard fashion devotees worshipped.

An hour later he came out laden with the latest in sexy menswear. He looked great in them, he had the word of the sales clerk on that. He had also preened in the changing room mirror and reckoned he looked pretty damn good. Being in fashion certainly altered a fellow. He looked taller and leaner.

Howard took to inventing appointments that enabled him to leave the office on nice sunny afternoons, change in the men's room, and parade himself in Central Park or on Fifth Avenue in his new clothes.

One day he spotted a reproduction poster for sale in a shop. It was of the Thirties matinee idol Ricardo Montalban. Howard reckoned Ricardo suited his new self very well, and adapted the name to Ricardo Monte. It must have been destiny because barely half an hour later he met the sexy lady he had seen in Macy's fashion department when he was boring old Howard.

As they passed each other Howard doffed his hat. Only super confident, sexy seducers doff their hats to a lady.

"Good afternoon," said Howard/Ricardo, as bold as you like behind his new persona, and Muriel/Zara smiled, cool and sexy in her new outfit. She was not wearing her new glasses, but she could see well enough that here was a dishy man.

He smiled suavely, and with the easy confidence of a man attired in top fashion fell into step beside her. Sexy seducers need very little small talk to get into action and he soon enquired: "What's your name?"

"Zara," she replied. "Zara Bow. What's yours?"

"Ricardo," he answered, "Ricardo Monte," and the name rolled off his tongue as smooth as you like. "Isn't it a beautiful day?"

"Wonderful!" agreed Zara.

It was love at first sight.

After that Zara soon ditched boring old Howard, and Ricardo walked out on boring old Muriel.

Neither felt guilty. Howard had convinced himself Muriel was having an affair. Muriel noticed that Howard looked uncharacteristically happy and concluded he had found himself a fancy piece.

It all worked out rather well, as the super confident Ricardo Monte was headhunted by a top finance house. He got a much bigger salary so he could afford Zara's expensive tastes - which indeed had become his own.

Ricardo did the decent thing. He left a note for their lawyer to give his half of the apartment to Muriel.

Zara felt a tiny twinge of conscience about deserting decent old Howard and left a note for their lawyer giving her half of their apartment to him.

The lawyer was confused but as he could not contact either Muriel or Howard he just sold the place and deposited the monies in their old joint account.

In their new affluent lifestyle neither Ricardo nor Zara noticed the extra money when they secretly transferred their share of the account into their new lives.

They adroitly got themselves passports and work permits for their new selves - with money and brains these things can be arranged.

Neither had cause to feel bad about leaving each other, as Zara learned her suspicions had been correct and Howard had indeed found someone. Ricardo too was right about Muriel and she had found herself a new man and was very happy.

While Ricardo loved all the wining and dining of his new life he was delighted to find that Zara was a wonderful cook and made him all his favourite meals. It was exciting, but also - he could not find a better word to express it - being with Zara was also *comfortable*.

The perfect couple, he would say to himself.

And Zara often thought how lucky she was to have a man as sexy as Ricardo who was also so dependable and *sensible*. We were meant for each other, she would tell herself as they snuggled up.

Thus Ricardo and Zara and Howard and Muriel lived happily ever after.

A Song for Lionel

A day off, and the sun was shining invitingly through the bedroom curtains. It was a 'sally forth and conquer the world!' kind of morning. Lionel Kenyon felt a song coming on and hummed as he made breakfast, trying to capture the tune that had been in his head when he awoke.

With a cup of coffee on top of the piano and slice of toast in one hand, he tinkled the keys one-handed trying to organise the notes and at the same time thinking of a lyric.

It was always like that when he had the muse. It was untidy, unorganised, and so far in his 30 years, unpublished. Sometimes he was annoyed with himself for not being more organised. His desk was stuffed with half finished songs that needed another think-about and any number of music manuscripts that had been rejected. One day he would look at them again and jiggle with them, then perhaps send them off to another publisher.

Was he was always going to be that sort of person, drifting along living his daydream of one day writing a chart-topper?

One day...I'm living in a dream...there was a song there and he ran his fingers over the piano keys seeking inspiration.

Then, damn! he knocked his coffee over and just managed to stop the spillage getting on to the piano keys with his shirt sleeve. By the time he had changed his shirt fickle muse had flown.

Oh well, the weather was fine so he got his cycle and went for a bowl into the countryside.

After a brisk ten-mile spin he arrived at Turnington, a pretty village beside the River Tain. Ready by then for a drink and bite to eat he stopped at the village pub. It was still early for lunch and the place was quiet. He ordered a beer and went out into the garden at the rear of the pub to sit beside the river.

"A lovely day."

Lionel looked round to see the only other person sitting in the garden was an elderly gentleman.

"Yes, beautiful," Lionel agreed. He indicated the river. "Nice place. I've been through this village a few times and never realised this beer garden was beside the river."

"My favourite place on a day like this. Lots of artists like to paint this section of the river."

"I can see why. Your favourite place? You come here often then?"

"Quite often. I live just down the road. River Cottage. Thirty years. Do you live locally?"

"Just outside Salisbury." Lionel extended his hand: "Lionel Kenyon."

The old man accepted it. "Frank Bennion."

Lionel supped his beer. "Ah, I needed that! Thirty years - you've settled here then!"

"Immovable. I was in local government. It paid the bills. You're not retired yet, I can see! What do you do for a living?"

"Surveyor. It pays the bills."

The old man smiled. "They have to be paid. Work interferes with dreams doesn't it."

"I suppose it does."

"Now I can spend all my time on my hobbies - well, hobby."

"Oh, what's that?"

"Well, I suppose you would call it a hobby. I write songs."

"Really? Well, I'm blessed. So do I!"

After that they got on like a house on fire and became good friends. Lionel was often invited to the cottage and listened to Bennion's songs played on the piano. Impressed - and secretly a little envious of their excellence - Lionel urged him to try and get them published. But the old man would only smile and shake his head.

"No, no. I prefer tinkering alone at home. They are just bits and pieces, not good enough for publishing," he said modestly.

"Too old now. I'm happy just to tinkle away at the piano. It's my hobby, my private pleasure. No one knows I write songs. At my age.... well, the quiet life suits me." The old man smiled shyly.

One afternoon Lionel asked: "What gives you your ideas? Is there a special place, a memory? Do situations or things inspire a song? Mine always come when I am half asleep in the early hours, but when I come to get them down on paper, they are never quite what I dreamed."

"The river," said the old man.

"The river?"

"Yes. I like to take my boat out and just paddle upstream, then drift back down. On a nice summer's day there's nothing to beat it. A day like today, for instance."

Suddenly he brightened. "Yes, like today. Come on, I'd like to show you something."

Wondering what he was about to see, Lionel followed the old man out of the back door of the cottage into an old-fashioned cottage garden. Beckoning Lionel to follow him along a garden path that ran between flower beds and vegetable plots the old man led him to a delightful spot.

"There," the old man pointed. Built by the look of it at least 50 years earlier was a boathouse and moored alongside a little jetty were a couple of rowing boats.

"When I need inspiration I take one of the boats out," said the old man. "Can't beat it. Out there, the imagination....expands, has room to think, as it were. You leave the world behind."

Then suddenly he suggested: "Let's go for a row now, there's room for two in the boat. Would you like to?"

Lionel was delighted. "What a nice idea. Love to!"

The old man started to untie the mooring rope then paused, looking at the river.

"Running a bit fast, after all that rain. But we'll be alright. Hop in."

The old man expertly sent the boat out into the river, and started to row upstream.

"Away from the weir," he said. "Then I coast back down. We'll reach a quiet backwater in a bit and take a rest."

But it quickly became apparent that the river was running faster than he had expected and despite his efforts they were being forced back downstream.

"Better get to the bank." the old man puffed. "It will be dangerous at the weir with this current."

Lionel was becoming alarmed as he heard the sound of the weir growing louder. He could see the old man was struggling to combat the river flow.

"Let me I row," he said. "I might be able to....."

"Alright!" The old man let Lionel take the oars. Then they tried to swap places but the swirling river swung the boat round and Lionel lost an oar.

Within moments the once-tranquil row on a river had turned into a nightmare as they flowed out of control towards the foaming weir.

In a normal flow with just a couple of inches depth of water going over the weir the boat would have bumped against the top and remained wedged. But today the river was too high and like a toy the boat toppled over the weir throwing them headlong into the swirling foam.

With lung-bursting slowness Lionel came to the surface and fought desperately to keep himself afloat. By good fortune he almost immediately found himself in a slowly eddying bend of the river where he managed to get to the bank.

But there was no sign of the old man or the boat.

Three days later the boat was found floating upside-down twelve miles downstream. Despite a week of searching by the authorities the old man's body was not found.

Lionel himself spent days searching the riverbank; not in any real hope but for the old man's memory. He had been a dear old chap and Lionel had come to be fond of him.

Then he remembered that the old man kept the key to his front door under a flower pot by the front door. With this thought Lionel was captured by the desire to revisit the cottage.

Inside was peaceful, exactly as they had left it. The kindly, mellow cottage accepted him as a friend. Lionel felt welcomed; at home.

Lionel sat in to the sunshine beside the boathouse and read the letter. He had used the key to River Cottage to return there whenever he liked. No one noticed his comings and goings. It was going to be some time before the old man's affairs were settled and the cottage sold. When it was, Lionel intended to buy it.

He did not quite know how to deal with his feelings as he read the letter. He had been right, the songs were publishable and he was delighted.

There was also a frisson of excitement and apprehension, like when he was lad and planning something naughty which would get him into trouble if he was found out.

To sound out whether the songs could be published for the old man Lionel had at first decided it would be simpler to send them to an agent in the old man's name. It had seemed a better idea than having to explain who he was, and what had happened. Getting them accepted was going to be very unlikely after all.

Then the unlikely had happened.

Dear Mr Bennion,

Music Masters are happy to publish your songs, the agent wrote, and they have already got two well-known singers, Tammie Love and Emmanuelle Rosa prepared to include four of them in their next albums.

Lionel had seen it as a way of doing something for old Bennion, respecting his memory. Hadn't he said more than once to the old chap that he ought to try and get them published?

Now what? It had been a good idea at the time, but now he had let himself in for a lot of work. What would happen regarding the royalties? The old man was dead.

They did not belong to anyone. Who ought to have them? That led to a train of thought that Lionel tried to resist. He, Lionel, had urged him to have the songs published; he, Lionel, had done his best for the old man when he was alive.

He, Lionel, deserved whatever financial rewards were forthcoming as much as anyone. There was no family, no dependants. No-one would be the loser.

The train of thought was irresistible. Lionel was swept along, out of control, much as he had been that afternoon on the river.

Jack Lemmon sat back and thought about the request.

"It's unusual, Mr Kenyon," he said finally. "Why do you want me to do it? It seems more like a music publisher's job."

"Not really. They just market the stuff. Oh, I just think that having you make up a contract, and registering me as the owner of the songs would be a safeguard. You read about so many people in the music business having problems over copyright. Famous names, millions of pounds…"

Lionel paused and tried a smile.

"Better safe than sorry. And, it's a little bit of business for you."

Lemmon grunted unappreciatively. A big bit of business was what he wanted. He was still reeling from the massive failure of a business venture he had invested in big, really big. All his eggs in one basket. Foolish, and he had paid the price of greed.

Nearly a million pounds, and he was practically on his uppers now. He would get back on track eventually, but he was still hurting.

"What made you decide on 'Frank Bennion?'"

"Oh, I prefer privacy. Otherwise, it would be what everyone you met talked to you about." Lionel smiled and shrugged. You know how it is.

In fact that was the only true thing he told the solicitor, as he did keep quiet about his song-writing. He had never wanted people to know he was not successful in getting any published.

Lionel pushed the music sheets across the desk to the solicitor.

"These are the songs, if you need to make a note of them."

Lemmon looked through them. "Fine, I'll get them copied."

Suddenly he looked sharply at one of the sheets.

"River Cottage in the Summertime, 1964? You wrote that in 1964?"

He looked quizzically at Lionel, who with a shock realised what he was thinking: that 1964 must have been before he was born.

Stemming the rise of panic Lionel concocted a hasty lie.

"Oh, I expect I was working on a song with a Sixties theme. Yes, yes I was, I remember now."

"I see," said Lemmon. The tone of his voice sounded sceptical to Lionel, who was still shaken by his carelessness at not noticing the date on the music sheet.

Ending the meeting Lemmon said: "We'll be back in touch."

Lionel left the solicitor's office distinctly unsettled, feeling he had rushed into this without enough forethought.

He pulled himself together. Don't worry, the solicitor had no reason to be suspicious. The old man had kept himself to himself about his song writing. Stop panicking!

For the next couple of days Lemmon was busy on other matters before he asked his clerk to bring Lionel's file. He had been looking through it for a several moments before he realised it was the wrong file.

Lemmon called the clerk back. "This is the wrong file William."

"Oh, sorry," William apologised. "Ah, yes, that's an old file on Frank Bennion of Turnington. Of course, Mr Kenyon's file also had Bennion written on it. My mistake, sorry."

Lemmon was about the hand the file back to the clerk to exchange for the right one when he spotted something that arrested his attention.

Frank Bennion, River Cottage, Turnington. The firm had acted for a Frank Bennion in the purchase of River Cottage in 1962.

River Cottage, that rang a bell.

"Very sad," said William as he took the file from Lemmon.

"Sad?"

"Yes, that was the chap who drowned on the river a few months ago. We have acted for him once or twice over the years. Nice old chap."

Now Lemmon became very interested. "Knew him? What was he like?"
"Oh, nice fellow. Didn't know him that well. He was a bachelor, I know that. He had no family. Yes, very sad." William left the office and returned with the correct file.

"I've filed it under Kenyon now," he said.

"Thank you," said Lemmon, but did not open the file. Instead he sat for a while thinking.

Just thinking....

Now he recalled the news story of the old man and the river drowning. There had been two men in a boat and one had drowned. Something about this was intriguing, and he got another clerk to get him a copy of the newspaper report on the accident.

And there it was: Kenyon. Lionel Kenyon. That was the name of the other man in the river drowning incident. A Lionel Kenyon had been the survivor.

Turning back to the file Lemmon checked through the music scripts until he found the one he was looking for: River Cottage in the Summertime.

Time to make further enquiries, and very quickly those enquiries confirmed that the owner of the cottage had been - still was - the same Frank Bennion. The date of Mr Bennion's birth was 1935, and he could well have been writing songs in 1964.

This Kenyon fellow certainly could not.

Now, how had Lionel come to have been involved in the boating accident with Bennion? Hmm. And how come he is now marketing songs as Frank Bennion?

Hmm. Very odd.

Very odd indeed.

Lemmon sat back in his chair, his devious mind working overtime. There could be something in this for him.

Over a drink at home that evening the solicitor set about reviewing the whole case.

As a citizen the solicitor knew he ought to go to the police. On the other hand as a citizen with a £1 million pound debt.....

By the time he had emptied half the bottle he had decided on his plan of action, a solution that would avenge poor Bennion - who he was now certain had been murdered by Kenyon - and at the same time solve his money problems.

If this Lionel Kenyon was going to make money from the songs he did not own, then why not someone else? Like someone with a £1 million debt?

Perfectly sound reasoning if you are a crooked solicitor.

Lionel Kenyon would soon be singing a sad song.

Meanwhile in River Cottage, where it now felt like his own home, Lionel was also doing some thinking.

Finally the elusive thing that had been niggling him since the solicitor's clerk had called him to check a detail suddenly came to him - Bennion! Mr Bennion? the clerk had enquired when Lionel answered the phone, correcting himself immediately with an apology.

"No, sorry - Mr Kenyon?" and had gone on to explain that the file had been filed under Bennion.

"You have a file on Frank Bennion?" With proper discretion William avoided answering that, but Lionel realised that the solicitor's office had a file on Frank Bennion for some reason and if the clerk had seen it so must the lawyer. By now he must realise that something was amiss.

Everything was going wrong.

However things started to go poetically right when the solicitor decided to drive out to River Cottage and have a nose around.

Things came to a perfect conclusion when Lionel arrived at the cottage at the same time and they bumped into each other.

After a few minutes of 'well I nevers' and bad acting on the part of both of them, Lionel invited the solicitor in, explaining his presence at the cottage with another hasty lie that he was renting the place.

Things finally came to a perfect conclusion when over a cup of coffee the solicitor looked along the garden to the boathouse and said: "Lovely day for a boat trip on the river."

"There's a boat in the boathouse," said Lionel. "Would you like to go for a little trip?"

"Love to," said the solicitor.

Within moments of crashing over the weir the old man became entangled in floating debris of plants and bits of trees. This raft of driftwood carried him downstream until it ended up eddying in a pool at a bend of the river where he was able to touch the river bottom and gain a foothold.

Slowly picking away the debris around him he was able at last to scramble ashore, trembling with cold and shock.

What had happened? Somehow he had fallen into the river, but what had happened? His mind was blank. The bank was sheltered and the sun was full on it, creating a vital warmth. He took off most of his wet clothing and sat with the sun beating on his back to allow the heat to get deep into him. In a mercifully short time he was warm again, and in an hour his clothes were dry enough to put on.

But what had happened? And, terrifyingly, who was he?

Mrs Wells was taking her dog for a walk when she saw the old man. At first she could not believe her eyes. Surely it must just be someone like him. She had to go up close, and stare him in the face before she was sure, and then she just stood there shocked, exclaiming over and again: "Mr Bennion! Mr Bennion! What happened? You're alive!"

When you meet someone who has come back from the dead it is difficult to stay calm.

Later, explaining it to neighbours she said: "I was just walking the dog, and had gone past his cottage and was actually thinking of him when, there he was! I thought it must be my imagination, having just been thinking of him. Oh, it was such a shock!"

The story was in all the papers. How the old man had been found wandering, having lost his memory.

"His recollection is coming back slowly," a spokesman for the social services said. "It will take some time for him to recall everything. Apparently he was taken to a hostel for the homeless, and no one realised who he was."

The old man himself could not remember anything about how he had ended up in the river, but somehow Turnington had lodged in his subconscious. Eventually he made his way there and Mrs Wells saw him.

The local newspaper sent a reporter to interview the old man when his recovery had progressed and his memory was beginning to return.

"An amazing story, Mr Bennion," he said. "How do you feel now about still living beside the river? It can be dangerous. Not long after you went missing two men also went over the weir in a boat and drowned."

"Yes, I was told about it, and then I remembered I knew one of them. Nice fellow."

With the help of neighbours the old man settled back into his life, and gradually more of his memory came back. He remembered his songs when he saw his old manuscripts again and playing them helped his recovery. Things fell into place, but there was one thing that that he could never recall doing.

A letter arrived from a music agent, telling him that his album of songs was selling well and now three artists had recorded four of them.

Goodness, thought the old man. I must have decided to get them published.

What a wonderful surprise.

Then he remembered that that nice young fellow Lionel had loved writing songs. Such a sad end for a young talent.

So he wrote a song in his memory and called it Lament for Lionel. It topped the charts.

She Married for Money

They say money is the root of all evil. On hearing that hoary old maxim Miss Jones would dismiss such silliness with her infectious no-nonsense laugh.

Money, evil? What does that make shopping at Harrods and Harvey Nicks - wicked? Shopping is heaven! Shopping is happiness and shopping needs money. Thus, money can buy happiness so how can money be evil?

The *lack* of money perhaps!

Our Miss Jones was not one to waste time on serious discussions, but when enjoying her company one would quickly realise that this lady had no morals regarding money. (She most certainly would not steal it, but maybe just coax it her way?)

It must be stressed that evil, or even nasty, was not in Miss Jones' nature. Far from it; she was a happy, fun-loving, good-hearted lady. The problem was that she had neither the desire nor the time (living as she did the full-time good life) or any qualifications to get a job. The closest to work she ever got were a few grace and favour appointments in her current boyfriend's business. Personal assistant was her usual job description, and her duties mostly entailed taking clients to lunch in the best restaurants.

These periods of employment were only occasional aberrations however as she had perfected the art of getting men to finance the fun-loving lifestyle her nature insisted upon.

Miss Jones was good company and never had trouble finding men to pick up the bill. With her expensive tastes they had to be men of financial substance, and it says much for Miss Jones' likeability that they paid up happily. Miss Jones was not a great beauty but was so sexy and such fun to be with that men loved her company. Sexy and fun. That's better than beauty and brains.

Marriage? Somehow with Miss Jones the question never arose. Miss Jones was not the sort of girl fellows married. Miss Jones was one of nature's natural-born mistresses. She was happy if a fellow bought her a ring - diamond, sapphire, opal; anything but wedding. Yes, men loved her. Anyway, if it was still the age when men made honest women of their women there would be a culpable queue miles long.

Not that any of this concerned our heroine. She was quite happy being single, with always a wealthy man to foot the bills.

Happy, that is, until one weekend middle-age arrived.

They say diamonds are a girl's best friend. Wrong. Youth is a girl's best friend. Diamonds are a middle-aged woman's best friend.

Miss Jones began to realise this that weekend when distressingly, and for the first time, she found herself without a well-heeled escort nor, indeed, with an invitation to spend the weekend anywhere.

It was a shock that focused her survival instincts.

It was time, she told herself, to find a rich husband.

With characteristic honesty Miss Jones knew that she would not be able to maintain married status for long, so her plan was simple; marry rich, divorce quickly and comfortably. These days a wife gets a hefty chunk of a husband's estate when they divorce, even after only a few months of matrimony.

As always, somewhere there is a Mr Right for a Miss Right, although it is sadly true that fate does not always arrange for them to meet each other.

However it did so this time, on a fateful evening.

It was a remarkable coincidence; quite amazing. But if one was discussing an event that defies belief, the sort of occurrence that makes one exclaim: "How on earth could ....?" One would realise that to arrive at the remarkable occurrence being discussed in those terms there would have had to have been a series of remarkable coincidences leading up to it. Life is made up of nothing but a series of coincidences is it not?

All coincidences are remarkable; they cannot be otherwise. They do not however always result in remarkable outcomes. However, this time fate was on form.

So on becoming acquainted with the following remarkable series of coincidences one does not have to suspend belief, only to accept that here and there in the melodrama of life an especially illogical farce will occur.

On this occasion fate decided on not just a 'Mr Right' but a Lord - Lord no less! - Right. Miss Jones was delighted, unaware that fate was in a mischievous mood, as into view toddled Lord Banratty.

As luck had it His Lordship was on the lookout for a wife, and being of no great age and reasonably presentable, he would normally have had little trouble in acquiring one. A title, high society and offering the potential Ladyship a berth at Banratty Castle in the Royal Shire of Bankshire should have made him a dead cert in the marriage stakes.

The snag was any potential Ladyship needed to have a very considerable fortune, because His Lordship was flat broke. Banratty Castle was in dire need of at least £5 million to halt the ancestral decay. A couple of elderly factotums remained and they only got paid because a few tourists were conned into parting with a fiver to look around the half a dozen rooms where what was left of the Banratty family heirlooms were on display.

Cold and draughty - experience how they lived in the 18th Century exhorted the brochure; damp - 'breathe in the smell of history!'

And the cakes in the tea room were never wasted if they were not all sold as they went on sale the next day as Victorian Workhouse Cakes. Very enterprising, but it was hard work and it was not stemming the tide of decay.

Lord Banratty's search for a wife was a reluctant expedition. He had always loved his bachelor life, but he had a great sense of family duty and the castle had been in the family for a thousand years. A rich heiress it had to be and resolutely, with a stiff upper lip, His Lordship set out for London on a mission to find one.

What happened next was extraordinary but extraordinary things do occur and money is often at the root of them.

It so happened that very soon both His Lordship and Miss Jones attended the same Knightsbridge do, the kind of place where Posh and Posers congregate to swap insincerity.

Of course neither His Lordship nor Miss Jones were what the other was looking for, but when people are in a hurry the oddest things happen. It was overhearing the word 'wealthy' that opened the curtain on the farce.

Lord Banratty heard it first and focused his attention in the direction that attractive and impossible to ignore word had come from.

Two ladies of leisure were nearby and his Lordship realised they were discussing the great wealth of a third lady.

"Her husband has just died and left her a packet," said one, and in so saying instantly had His Lordship's undivided attention.

From the way they were peering discreetly as they discussed this lady's wealth - which ran into millions they were saying - she was nearby. Eagerly His Lordship craned to see who it could be.

"Who is she?" one lady enquired of her friend

"There, her in the blue dress and that chiffony thing round her neck," replied the other, nodding discreetly towards the woman in question.

With a neat sidestep learned on the playing fields of Eton His Lordship changed position to be able to see who it was she was indicating.

Now it was at this point that fate played the first of its tricks. Quick as his footwork was, the wealthy widow had melted into the crowd. Quite remarkably, and this, if you know anything at all about the mischiefs of fate, you will have no difficulty in believing, Miss Jones had been behind the wealthy widow and His Lordship's eager eye alighted on her instead. Even more remarkably, she was wearing a blue dress and a chiffony thing round her neck.

By itself, one remarkable coincidence was not enough. Just one and Miss Jones would have encouraged the noble lord's attentions, and have had the time to suss out his attractions. Then, realising as she would inevitably have done, that His Lordship was not able to afford to court such a spendthrift as herself for even a fortnight without the bailiffs entering Banratty Castle Miss Jones would have turned her attention elsewhere.

However - in these plots of human farces there is always an 'however' - it so happened that at the very same time Miss Jones overheard another conversation nearby between another two ladies. Their conversation also consisted, as these London society conversations generally do, of the analysis of the personal wealth of all the other posers.

And 'he's loaded' fell sweetly upon Miss Jones' ear.

"Who is?" she heard one lady enquire of the other.

"Him with the beard wearing the dark blue jacket," replied her companion, indicating an ancient gent tottering nearby on a stick. "Worth half a billion they say."

Her attention thus riveted Miss Jones edged to see whose money the two gossiping ladies - always the ladies of course, City men discuss race horses and stocks and shares - were talking about.

At this same moment Lord Banratty was craning to see who the other two ladies had been discussing and stepped into her line of sight, stroking his beard and looking quite prosperous in a smart dark blue jacket.

"Absolutely loaded," went on the lady who knew everyone's business. "No one to leave it to when he dies!"

Thus was the moment His Lordship's search was over and Miss Jones' dreams were realised.

Or so they thought.

In the normal course of events both Miss Jones and Lord Banratty would have realised their mistakes. As has already been pointed out, Miss Jones spent money like water, and little more than a week of courting her would have stretched His Lordship's finances to breaking point. It would also have become obvious to His Lordship that Miss Jones was not a wealthy widow.

On her part Miss Jones would have soon started wondering why a man said to be worth millions lived in a castle where the roof leaked in several places and the servants (only two) earned their wages conning a thin straggle of visitors.

However His Lordship, for the very reason of being broke, was in a hurry and Miss Jones, impetuous creature that she was and the painful memory fresh in her mind of the lost weekend, decided to grab the chance while he was, as it seemed to her, smitten by her charms and she was still no more than middle-aged.

Her quickly hatched plan was marriage, a quick divorce, a nice settlement, and no worries. He thought he had won the lottery.

So he proposed and she said yes!

They were hitched by special licence within the week.

Of course the matter of money had to come up sometime, sooner than later as far as His Lordship was concerned, and with remarkable delicacy, a delicacy that comes from centuries of good breeding, the matter was broached.

It was at breakfast that His Lordship, after a few skirmish noises such as mmmm, hurrumph and 'I wonder, old girl', asked the new Her Ladyship could she, er, could she, hurrumph, stump up a little something to pay the man delivering the cartridges for the guns? A jolly old pheasant shoot this afternoon, you see. Just £2,000 should do it, plus that already owing the man. Temporary hiccup with funds, you know. Blasted nuisance and all that but ...

It took less than five minutes over the soft-boiled boiled eggs and toast for the whole remarkable cock-up to finally be plain to both of them as boggle-eyed questions and increasingly incredulous replies were bandied back and forth.

Neither finished their breakfast, and the cartridge man never got paid.

Her Ladyship fled back to London where she still had kind friends on whose shoulders she could cry, and in whose beds she was still welcome.

"He deceived me," she told them, all of whom were sympathetic to this fun-loving woman.

"I want half the estate!" she demanded through her solicitors.

Gold digger! That's what Lord Banratty's friends dubbed her in a spirited defence of the old boy.

"I married him for love, but all he wanted was money," responded Her Ladyship through her solicitor. His Lordship's refusal to keep her in the style she to which was accustomed amounted to cruelty.

In the ensuing divorce proceedings she staked claim to half the Banratty estate which, although impoverished, sold off would still realise a tidy little sum filled with bungalows or a theme park.

But fate was still in its mischievous mood. It so happened that a long-forgotten auntie - in the best farces it is always a long-lost auntie - on hearing that her niece, of whom she had always thoroughly disapproved, had become a Ladyship was so shocked, and perhaps a teeny bit jealous, she promptly passed away. It was sad, but not quite the tragedy it might otherwise have been as the auntie in question was 99 and the end was quick while snoozing in her armchair after a tot of her favourite tipple.

Not expecting to die so young she had omitted to make a will and with no other relatives her fortune of £40 million went to her niece.

Then for good measure fate arranged for the six numbers Her New Ladyship had picked the previous Saturday might in the lottery - a habit of a lifetime - to come up and she won a handy £10 million.

When the parties met with their lawyers to finalise the divorce paperwork Lord Banratty looked over the legal documents on the solicitor's desk at Her Ladyship and enquired with a very large smile: "A settlement for half, did you say old girl?"

After a little bargaining His Lordship graciously settled for £20 million. There was no animosity. Miss Jones - now known socially as Her Ladyship - had a sense of humour and could see the funny side of it all, and she and His Lordship remained good friends. Occasionally they would meet for lunch, and without having all the trials and tribulations of being married, His Lordship had his batteries recharged with a blast of Her Ladyship's jollity, and returned to Banratty Castle good for another three months. No one to nag him and the staff got paid regularly.

Her Ladyship enjoyed a whole new lease of fun in a Chelsea flat of her own with both money and a title. There is nothing quite like money and title to make a lady's mature years comfortable. Indeed the title was worth more than the money, as she discovered that it opens more posh doors than do wallets.

Everyone happy, thanks to money.

So, should you run into Her Ladyship on London's society circuit, and enquire of her philosophy regarding money, she will treat you to her cheerful chortle and tell you it is only the root of all evil when it runs out.

Son of the Ripper

She heard him downstairs.

He had crashed into furniture and was swearing: the usual torrent of foul oaths when he was drunk. Hastily she got out of bed to give him his meal.

Before going down she checked that their son's bedroom door was closed. If he started beating her, which was usual when he came out of the pub angry drunk, she did not want the boy to hear.

He was slumped at the kitchen table when she got downstairs.

"Where's m' bloody dinner?"

"It's in the oven. I 'll get it."

She put it on the table with a glass of beer. He always had a glass with his dinner, no matter how much he had drunk during the evening. If she forgot he got angry.

She sat while he ate and drank, ready to give him some more if he asked.

Except for the crass sound of his eating and drinking, the room was silent. It was the silence of emptiness. Like her life.

Then from the street came the raucous voices of drunkards leaving taverns. The voices got louder, excited. Then she heard one shout: "'E's done anuvver one. The Ripper's ripped anuvver 'ore."

Amid the cacophony a woman screamed.

"'Urry 'ome gel," a coarse voice shouted, "before 'e gets yer!"

This was greeted with raucous laughter.

She looked across the table and saw he had been listening and there was a grin - a savage twist of his lips - on his face. Her hatred of him was a routine hatred, weighing down, destroying her soul. Seeing his ugly expression made it boil up.

A defenceless woman is slaughtered; a slut maybe but still a human being, and he…he smirks! She shuddered and sat silent. He finished eating, belched loudly, and went up to bed.

She cleared the table and waited a while before following him. Thankfully he was already in a snoring drunken sleep. She lay down as far from him as she could, and fell into a dream in which she was young and happy.

Early next morning she got up and made the boy's breakfast before he set off for school. She watched him eat it. If it was not for him she would have run away years ago. He was a quiet, introspective boy. He always got good exam results.

"He takes after me, has my brains," his father once boasted when someone remarked on the boy's school results. It was a rare occasion when he took any notice of his son, who had his father's looks, his dark eyes.

She packed his sandwiches and walked with him to the school gates. She bent to kiss him goodbye, but he turned away. Getting too big to be seen by his friends being kissed, she thought, suppressing a mother's hurt at his rejection. Not that he had any friends.

On her way back home the newspaper vendors were shouting out the latest Ripper killing. When she arrived home he had bought a paper and was reading about the murder. When she gave him his breakfast he was still reading the story.

She remembered him weeks before studying the latest Ripper stories and he had left several old newspapers on his bedside table, all about the killings. He had cut out some reports that dealt with the grisly details of body parts being cut out of the women. He had trained to be a surgeon and worked in the Free Hospital for a short while until drink got him.

She recalled the look on his face the night before when he was listening to the crowd in the street. As she did the housework, it kept running through her mind.

'e's dun anuvver one. The Ripper's ripped anuvver 'ore!

Lunchtime as usual he went down the pub. She went to the market to get some food. Everyone was talking about the murder.

"Those poor wimmin," said a woman in a crowd discussing the murders. "When are the bloody rozzers goin' ter catch 'im, eh?"

"They take the risks. They're prostitutes," sneered a man unsympathetically.

"No matter what they are, they don't deserve that," another woman snapped at him.

"They're all God's creatures, no matter wot," said another. "It's you men cause 'em to take risks! I know one woman oo's 'usband beats 'er and makes 'er go on the streets. 'E's a bloody pig!"

"Yeah," said another woman. "Men that beat their missus should be dun in, the bloody lot of 'em! They cause all the misery in this world!"

The man guffawed, and acted scared.

"I wouldn't wanna be married to you, luv! You'd 'ave me 'ead orf!"

She walked on as the group cackled with mirth.

Men that beat their missus should be dun in, the bloody lot of 'em'!

Again she recalled the look on his face the night before when listening to the crowd in the street.

"'E's dun anuvver one. The Ripper's ripped anuvver 'ore!"

That night he came home drunk, and this time he did not like his dinner. He threw it across the table at her. Something snapped, and she screamed.

"I 'ate yer! 'Ate yer! 'Ate yer!"

He came at her like a madman, fists flailing and knocked her senseless. That was fortunate, as when she was down he stopped, otherwise in the savage mood he was in he would likely have killed her.

Then he stumbled up to bed and fell asleep right away.

When she recovered consciousness she had a cup of tea, and sat for a while reflecting on her life. Then she followed him.

'Men that beat their missus should be dun in, the bloody lot of 'em'.

He never woke up again.

In the morning she walked to the school as usual with her son. On her way back she left a note at the convent. On her way to meet him in the afternoon she left another note at the police station, telling the desk sergeant to pass it on to his superior right away.

When she got back home with the boy the police were waiting for her. In the kitchen where she had spent so many soulless hours they arrested her and charged her with the murder of her husband. They started to escort her out of the house.

"Let me say goodbye to my son," she pleaded.

"Be quick," they said.

She hugged the boy and kissed him.

"They will look after you," she said. "Always remember your mother loves you." He showed no emotion. The last image she carried away with her was the dark void of his eyes.

Exactly like his father's. Her heart froze.

At the Old Bailey she was sentenced to death, but on appeal her husband's brutality was taken into account and the sentence was commuted to 20 years.

She wrote to her son every week, but never got a reply.

The duty sergeant at Barking police station put his head round the door of the Superintendent's office

"Another murder, sir."

The Superintendent held up his hands.

"Not another! That will make six in the past two months. The killings of these prostitutes are making unwelcome headlines for Barking in the gutter Press."

"It's not another prostitute sir," the sergeant answered. "This time it's a man. Mortimer Street."

"A man? Perhaps a prostitute got her revenge." He did not smile. It was a bad joke.

"Not this time, sir. Details just coming in, but it seems he was killed by his mother."

"His mother?"

"We are at the house now. His wife called us in. She told officers that a few days ago a woman had 'come out of the blue' as she put it, saying she was her husband's mother. They let her stay, and then she killed him. Stabbed him to death while he was asleep.

"Then she just waited in the house until she was arrested."

* * * * * * * * * * * * * * *

The Barking police were holding a meeting about the prostitute killings.

"There have been none for six months," reported the Inspector in charge of the enquiry team. "We have no fresh leads. It means the chances of catching him are zero, unless he starts again and is caught red handed."

"We will just have to wait and see," agreed the Superintendent. "The pattern of these types of killings is that they often suddenly stop – remember the Ripper murders, 20 years ago in Whitechapel? They suddenly ended. No known reason. They just stopped.

"Let's hope they have this time."

He moved on to other matters.

"That woman, the mother who killed the man she said was her son, hangs today.

"At least that was a simple case. But very weird. She admitted it, but would not explain why."

The station sergeant said: "I have checked on her records, sir. She also admitted she murdered her husband and got life. Just like this killing, she confessed to it. That was back in the East End, 1880's. Her son was taken into care, raised by nuns in an orphanage. No doubt she would have killed him then if she had not been arrested. Must be mad, or wicked."

"What on earth made her track him down after all these years, just to kill him?"

The sergeant shrugged. "Some things are beyond explanation."

The Superintendent nodded agreement.

"Never ends. Never ends. Another widow, another family on the parish – did he have any kids?"

"Just one son."

"Poor little sod."

He closed the meeting

The Temporary End

The Café of Your Dreams

All Henry's friends were squashed into the little seaside café where he had spent 40 years of his life serving teas and snacks to generations of holidaymakers.

The Mayor was there, together with leading townsfolk. They all wanted to be there for this special occasion.

It was six months since Henry had died, and his friends had clubbed together to have a portrait of him put up in his old café. The elderly couple who had bought the café when Henry became ill thought it a good idea and had given their permission.

The picture was covered ready to be unveiled by The Mayor and while they waited everyone had a tale to tell about the popular Henry, who had been involved in so much of the town's life.

They all clapped when the picture was unveiled, and there was Henry's amiable face gazing down on his old friends.

Ted Collier, one of his friends, laughed because it captured perfectly Henry's habitual twinkling expression; always on the verge of a wink and a chuckle.

"That's him, that's old Henry to a T," he said. "You always felt cheered up around Henry."

His companions, Tom Smith, Billy Venney and Charlie Barnes agreed.

Up on the wall Henry looked down and smiled to himself, tickled pink that they had no idea that he was watching and listening.

Ted raised his glass to the portrait.

"To you Henry. Bachelor to the end! Goodness! Do you know? I swear he just winked at me. How odd."

Tom chuckled. "Typical Henry. He always did enjoy mystifying people."

"Into everything weird, wasn't he," said Charlie. "The occult, clairvoyance, time travel. Reckoned there were different layers of existence that we can live at the same time."

Henry looked smug. Well, I was right, wasn't I? And here I am to prove it!

"You know," said Billy, "I don't know anyone more involved with people than Henry was."

Everyone had something nice to say about Henry.

"Always ready to help if he could, was Henry," said Cllr Brown.

Henry smiled modestly.

"Involved in everything," said Charlie.

"Don't know how he managed to run his café as well," said The Mayor.

"Never married, did he," said Tom.

"Not for want of women who would have married him," said Ted.

Henry looks modest.

Billy nodded agreement. "There was one in particular, wasn't there? Sally – I forget her surname."

Henry remembers her all too well but not happily judging by his expression.

Lizzie, who had worked as a waitress at the café for years, knew the answer having enjoyed the gossip at the time.

"Sally White. But she had a hard job pinning him down. Henry liked his freedom too much - and his sport."

Henry nods agreement to that, as he recalls himself flying down the wing, cutting inside one, two, three defenders and scoring a brilliant winner in the last minute of time in the village league cup final. Cheering villagers carry him off shoulder high.

"Yes, she certainly had her sights on Henry," said Lizzie.

Henry remembers the party in the village hall to celebrate the victory and the one of the girls serving tea is Sally.

'Time you were wed', one of the older tea ladies says to Henry, and you can see Sally is thinking: 'yes - to me!'

'Not me, I like my freedom,' asserts Henry.

'Some girl will change your mind one day' vows the tea lady. 'Don't you want to marry and have a nice family?'

'No, it's a bachelor's life for me!' chortles our laddo.

The tea lady, who knows how Sally feels, advises her kindly: 'Better look elsewhere love.'

But you can see from Sally's expression that she is not giving up that easily!

Billy was rummaging through his memory. "There was a bit of a scandal wasn't there?"

Henry winces. Don't bring that all up again!

"Yes," said Lizzie, now thoroughly enjoying all that old gossip. "Finally he succumbed, and he and Sally were going to be wed, but he jilted her at the altar.

"Apparently he went out with the lads the night before and overslept.

Had a bit too much to drink."

Henry looks glum as he too remembers. There he is staggering up the church path, only to meet a furious Sally flouncing the other way. Standing there looking stupid, Henry is subjected to a furious tirade from Sally's mother.

Billy, typical male chauvinist, grunted sympathetically. "Don't blame him. He must have needed a drink to stiffen his resolve. I know her, she's a bit of a tartar."

Henry nods emphatic agreement, recalling how he followed Sally, but when he got to her house she threw her wedding bouquet at him.

"She is now, perhaps, but not when she was young," said Lizzie. "All the fellows used to chase her, but she was set on Henry. But he preferred being a bachelor."

Billy was more interested in Henry's weird theories.

He asked Ted: "What were you saying about Henry and time travel?"

"Parallel existence, something like that. Enabling people to go back and live in the past." Ted grinned and shrugged. "That was how he put it to me when I asked him about his ideas. He chuckled when he saw the look on my face!"

Billy laughed. "But the past is the past! Gone!"

"Henry did not think so," said Ted. "'No, it hasn't - how can it not exist?' he always answered. 'It happened, it must still be there, somewhere. All you need to find a way to find it.' Baffled me, I can tell you!"

"Hmm," mused Billy, "I suppose when you think about it, if it happened, it existed - it happened so it's….somewhere…"

Ted laughed and dug Billy in the ribs. "He's converting you - if he is looking down on us he would be pleased to hear you say that. Life is all a dream, he used to say."

Henry nods. That's the secret. You can go back in your dreams, without altering the present.

"Time travel in a dream. Crazy! He tried to explain it to me once. But it was beyond me."

Henry shrugged: well I tried!

Ted laughed. "Lovely bloke. He told me that some people go back to be someone they were in the past - in the mind. That way you did not alter the past, because that could not be altered."

Henry nods, that's about it.

"Henry said it is a state of mind in which you relive the past as you wanted. A dual existence.

Ted shook his head. "I told him he was nuts!"

That makes Henry smile, and he recalls the conversation.

Ted is shaking his head, baffled.

"Henry, how can you live the past as you want - it's gone!"

"No it's not," says Henry patiently. "Otherwise, you would not be able to remember it. It has passed by, but it is still there. If it's gone, how can you still remember it? Nothing's gone. It is all one, the past, the present."

Ted protests. "But if you change the past for something else, what about all the people then? They're wiped out, never existed? That's not right!"

"No, no. They still happened, but your other life will exist in parallel!"

Ted just laughed. "You're nuts Henry! And what about the future?"

"I don't know. There is no future before it happens. So there may not be future, eh? Nobody knows. Nobody can prove it, can they? There may not be a future, just a constantly changing now."

"You're living in a dream world Henry!"

"Well, didn't Shakespeare say this is all dream? This dream we call reality is the most vivid for most people, but who is to say which dream is real, or that you can't live another at a different time?"

"Like I said Henry, you're nuts!"

Ted looked up at Henry's picture. "I never understood. Perhaps I was the one who was nuts Henry. Maybe you are in your own dream world now." He raised his glass: "Let's hope so!"

Another guest agreed. "I wonder where he is now?"

"I wonder. Helping the angels with their problems!"

Henry is amused. No, nothing that grand!

With a final toast to their old friend, everyone left the café smiling. That was the effect Henry had on people.

After they had all gone a woman entered the cafe and after looking around it for a few minutes, looked up at Henry's picture. Anyone looking at the portrait would have sworn Henry had a worried expression. Another trick of the light? But the look on Sally White's face as she glared up at Henry was no trick of the light.

She was remembering being jilted.

Henry looks relieved when Sally leaves the café. But he is puzzled, wondering why she had come,

The next morning dawned a new day. Now Henry was ready to put into practice what he had always believed; that it was possible to travel in time and live another life. With more time to reflect and analyse existence since his departure from the material world he had refined his theories. He had connected somehow to the force within him to travel in the mind, and now he was ready to start.

I could never explain it properly when I was alive, but we can travel back in time via our dreams. It is obvious that dreams are not made of the same material as, say, our physical bodies, so different physics must apply. What makes dreams a way to the past is not explainable. It just works and if you connect, you connect. Trying to work out why just leads you round in circles. Just believe. In our dreams we can do anything and be anything we want. It is being able to direct those dreams that elude us. I can direct your dreams from here, and you will live the times you want, and the effect on you will be real, but not physical. Here and now will always be the same, but in your spirit, your inner self, you will have done or seen or resolved whatever you wanted to. How it happens do not ask me, I do not know. Just believe.

Henry then settled down to a happy afterlife realising his own dream - enabling people to realise theirs.

However, in the town Sally was busy doing some business negotiations.

Henry was soon busy. In the first week of being on the wall he sent a retired police Inspector back in time to investigate famous unsolved murders, and the Inspector enjoyed it so much he opted to stay in limbo to become The Time Detective, investigating all the famous, but often unknown murders in history.

Another café dreamer was sent back to join Robin Hood's Merry Men, and enjoys a right set-to with the Sherriff of Nottingham and he flirts (dangerously!) with Maid Marion.

By midweek he had sent a man back to dine at a banquet with Henry the 8th and is able to prevent an attempt to kill him, an incident that does not get into the history books. (He is rewarded with a night with a tasty lady-in-waiting. She teaches him a thing or two!)

A film producer goes back to take a stroll with Charles Dickens round London, discussing his latest books, and then makes a film of it.

A Cambridge professor enjoys a trip back to discuss philosophy face to face with Aristotle – and she gives Aristotle a few ideas to mull over. Surprisingly the philosopher turns out to be a ladies man and she comes back with more than philosophic memories.

An amateur author and enthusiast of Charlotte Bronte novels goes back to meet her in Holworth and goes for a moorland hike with her to discuss how to write a novel. She ends up in an adventure that gives her an idea for an award-winning novel – My Adventure with Charlotte Bronte.

All the time travellers came back knowing more about famous people from the past than any history book could tell them. For example as he surveyed the café patrons one morning, wondering what today would bring Henry heard a group of men in jocular mood, and one says, "I bet the beauties you read about were not half as gorgeous as they are made out to be - artists and poets have done a public relations job on them I bet."

"Nell Gywnne sounds a right tasty lass," chips in his mate. "She must have had something special, for a king to choose a call girl, because that is what she was."

Henry notices one of the men is smiling to himself. Henry tunes in and the man is thinking it would be fun to have an affair with Nell.

Henry reflects a minute and then thinks: why not? He would be one of many, so it would not alter history.

Later the men are back in the café. The man who went to see Nell said, "She was not a whore as most people think of her. She was a lovely young lady, and it was no wonder King Charles loved her. Every man - real men - who met her loved her. If all women were like her, there would be no more wars, no more crime, because every man would be content."

His mates stare at him in surprise. "And how come you know so much about Nell Gywnne? You've studied her it seems."

"Yeah, closely. History books don't always get it right." And the man winks.

So does Henry.

One morning Henry was listening to the chatter of the customers when he overheard a conversation between a group of men, all former soldiers.

One of them was saying to the others: "I would like to be able to travel back and see how it really was to serve under those fabled warlords of history. I was reading about Rameses the Great and his battles.

"The tales of ancient warlords told and re-told down the ages have become mythical. I would love to be able to experience them personally."

"But if you did, you would be dead!" laughed his friends.

Henry saw that the man really meant what he said, and after a moment's reflection, thought, that sounds just right for this old solider, so why not?

And the old soldier then started off on his journey in time, seeing in action such Titans and Tyrants as Rameses the Great , Sun Tzu, Caesar, Caligula, Nero, Richard I I, Catherine the Great, David and Solomon, and Napoleon I I I.

When the café closed that evening Henry felt it had been a very satisfying day.

Henry is enjoying himself, but gets a scare one day. A group on holiday are talking about their day out along the coast to Charmouth to a dinosaur museum.

"I'd love to back in time and see one of them close up," says one of the men. "They might eat you" jokes his wife, and they all laugh.

Henry smiles and grants his wish.

The next day the holidaymakers are back in the café but he is not with them. One of says: "I read they found a man's skeleton among dinosaur bones in a cliff fall at Charmouth. They reckon the dinosaur ate the man and he choked on it."

Henry looks alarmed. Then the man hurries into the café, "Got caught up in a queue at the till," he explained.

Henry's expression is 'phew!'

Henry is enjoying himself and discovers that the world is full of dreamers. Every day he is busy. In his next week on the wall he hears an actor wishing: "Just once I would love to act on stage at the Globe alongside Will Shakespeare, and maybe some of his genius will rub off on me." Henry duly obliges him.

A retired Army general is sent back to take in the Battle of Hastings and a sailor gets the chance to serve on Nelson's flagship at the Battle of Trafalgar.

Henry had just finished sending a man back to Paris during the Uprising when into the café comes Sally.

She glares up at Henry and says triumphantly. "I have bought the café Henry. It's mine now!"

Henry's expression is 'oh dear!'

A little girl is looking up at the picture. "Mummy, that man keeps making faces!"

"What? Who is?"

The girl points to Henry who quickly composes his face.

"Oh that's just a picture dear. It's just the light, silly!"

Sally heard what the child said. "Don't worry, love," she says. "I'm taking the picture down tomorrow." So saying she glares up at Henry with grim satisfaction. "I'm taking you down Henry, and I have bought a nice picture to replace you!"

First thing the next morning when the café opened a van arrives and the driver brings in new picture. "It's going up there," Sally tells Daphne and Lizzie the waitresses.

"What, you're taking poor old Henry down?"

"Never mind 'poor old Henry'. He's coming down!"

When Sally went off to oversee the kitchen Daphne looked up at the picture. "You should have married her Henry!"

Lizzie stoutly defended Henry. "What bloke would want to marry someone like her?"

Henry nodded in agreement.

"Well, you had your chance Henry," said Daphne. "You can't change the past."

Oh yes I can thinks Henry, and he screws up his face, concentrate, connects to his new powers and:

Young Sally (having just been asked by Henry to marry him) 'Oh yes, Henry, of course I will. I thought you would never ask!'

Glumly Henry leads her up the aisle and they wed. Eventually, after spending right to the last minute at the honeymoon hotel bar an unenthusiastic Henry slowly makes his way to the honeymoon bed.

Then, lo and behold! we see Henry next morning coming down all smiles.

Back to present: Sally, looking now much more mellow and attractive, after a life of marital bliss, looks up at Henry's picture.

"'Night, 'night Henry darling. See you in my dreams. It was a lovely marriage, wasn't it?"

Henry nods, beaming.

"Remember how shy you were? I thought you would never pop the question! I'm glad you did, aren't you?"

Henry nods. Yes!

Sally blows him a kiss. "Nothing's changed Henry dear. We are still a partnership, and we'll make this café a place to where other people can be as happy as us, right?"

Henry nods again emphatically. He looks around at the people sat at the tables. Everything is all right now folks. Sally will make sure nothing goes wrong.

We'll make your dreams come true!

And perhaps he will make yours come true, if you are lucky enough to find the Café of Your Dreams.

Freddy Fogg's Rebellion

It was actually a major act of rebellion, a seismic upheaval in the well-ordered routine of Freddy Fogg's life. Rather annoyingly however, it went without Doris, his wife of umpteen years, noticing.

It was rather like that time when a picture fell off the living room wall. Freddy had been quietly reading the morning newspaper when the picture fell down. It had hung there for years and years; then it just decided it had hung there long enough and crashed to the floor.

It must have been something like that with Freddy this morning after 40 years of the same routine. There was nothing the slightest bit different from any of a thousand such mornings following Doris up and down supermarket aisles.

But suddenly he just pushed the trolley towards her and said; "Here, you can do without me. I'll wait for you in the café."

However Doris missed this act of independence as she was busy at the time working out which was the best buy: Tesco own brand tins of baked beans in tomato sauce at 2x 125g for 22p or Heinz 150g for 14p.

As rebellions go it was not very spectacular and certainly not as fundamental as Freddy would have wished, but the truth was that in his life there was not much else to rebel against. For a pensioner who was beginning to ponder the meaning of life his rebellion was decidedly unsatisfactory.

Worse, as he sat in the café among other pensioners reading the free newspapers and agonizing about his life, he saw Doris walk straight by without seeing him. When he caught her up at the car she looked surprised.

"I thought you were waiting in the car," she said.

"I said I would be in the cafe!"

"Oh, did you," she replied abstractedly as they emptied the contents of the shopping trolley into the car.

"I was with you, pushing the trolley, and I said I would see you in the cafeteria!"

"Oh, did you? Their cauliflowers are dear this week."

It was bad enough being a rebel without a cause, but a rebel that is not even noticed!

Freddy sighed.

At the pub he expected sympathy from fellow husbands who also did the weekly traipsing round supermarkets pushing trolleys. As a born-again non-conformist he was filled with oracular fervour,

"People will drive up and eat an all-day breakfast for 99p with only the car park for scenery. Then they traipse round the supermarket, homing in on every penny off, 50 per cent extra, buy one get one half price, special offer. Then they buy them whether they really need them or not.

"That's the women, and their husbands trot along behind pushing the trolley. They are like milkmen's horses, following exactly the same routes week after week along the same aisles and stopping automatically - without the need for a 'whoa there!' – at the right place. The only variety they get is if the supermarket decides to change the place it puts its potatoes or tins of beans or whatever. Then the poor chap has to follow his complaining missus up and down the aisles until she finds the blessed things."

Freddy paused for their agreement.

"That reminds me," said Ted Black. "They reckon Asda is doing a special offer on beer, eight cans for the price of six."

Freddy sighed.

It was half past seven and Asda closed at eight. The men felt the call of adventure and to a man rushed off with Ted to grab some of that bargain beer before the supermarket closed.

Freddy was left alone to listen to Mrs Bellows at the next table telling her companions that Tesco was doing a special offer on Kelloggs cornflakes, buy one packet, get one half price. That started a lively five-minute discussion on the rival offers in Safeway.

Freddy sighed.

Mrs Bellows glared at him. "What's up with you Freddy Fogg? What are you sighing about?"

"Nothing's up," muttered Freddy testily, and fell silent. Truth was he did not really know what he was sighing about, except that he had reason to sigh.

Freddy knew that if he wanted to juice up his life, it was up to himself. His head told him plainly enough. He was not arguing. It was just that somewhere along the thousand years he had lived in this vale of consumerism he had become a helpless supermarket junkie.

What had started out as an inviting road leading to the village shop for a bag of sweets, and later to exciting town centre shops, had become a motorway to boring shopping barns.

Freddy was only now beginning to realise it, but what he had always thought of as the real world was now only in books and old films of a far-off and long-ago England.

The real world was motorways and concrete. You left work to sleep in a brick box in another area of concrete in order to be refreshed to return to work the next morning to the section of concrete you left the evening before.

Now that he had retired his world was shopping. He slept in a brick box, took Doris shopping, and returned to the brick box. That was it. A bit of gardening but with size of the garden that goes with a house these days that took two minutes a month.

The real world was Consumerland.

"We're going to Pickerings," said Doris. "Are you ready?"

Pavlov would have been excited at the sight of Freddy, who had no idea until then that they were going shopping, automatically getting out of his chair and putting his coat on. Pavlov only had dogs on which to test his theories of auto-reaction. Nowadays he has millions of hapless husbands like Freddy.

Parking was free at the supermarket but Pickerings was in town where they charged for parking so they took the bus. But this time it was not just another shopping trudge in the life of Freddy. It was in Pickerings that he discovered his destiny.

While Doris shopped Freddy sat down in an armchair in the furniture department to test it for comfort. Sitting there he experienced the feeling that explorers have felt when standing alone on a vast plain, or gazing out from the top of a great mountain. Somehow he knew, just knew, that he had discovered a new world. This was where he must stay. This was his destiny.

Doris shopped on and did not realise he was no longer with her. When the store closed and the lights dimmed he kept his head down. The sales assistants closed up their tills and could be heard calling goodnight to each other as they departed. Nobody appeared to be looking for him; Doris may not have even remembered he came with her. She may have been puzzled for a moment and then caught the bus back home. Later when the night security people patrolled he moved to a less visible spot. The check was perfunctory and he was not spotted. It was all so simple.

He felt he had stepped sideways into a different life zone. Perhaps he was invisible. But of course he was still in the real world, except that now the real world had become Pickerings Department Store. He had become a naturalised Pickering.

That first night he found a bed in the bed department, borrowed a duvet and settled down for a lovely night's sleep. He was up bright and early the next morning, smoothed down the bed and returned the duvet. By the time the staff arrived he was in the café getting some breakfast.

The night security was provided by a rota of several men and Freddy just became accepted as someone who worked at the place.

Freddy was amazed at how complete his life was in the store. It catered for everything 'from birth to death' as the staff joked as there was a baby department and an undertaker service.

After a while, before the spare money he had on him ran out, he managed to get his name on a list in the office for free meal vouchers to use in the staff canteen.

The staff room had very nice clean toilets and a shower adjacent to the sports room. The staff soon got used to seeing him around. There was no need to lie about who he was. He told them his name and just made himself useful, first on one floor then another. A disused cupboard became his little office and he installed tea-making facilities for an evening cuppa.

Within a short while he became one of those general all-purpose people who just drift through every large organization. At night he slept in the showroom beds and by day ate at the staff canteen. But he paid his way by work, and whenever he needed new clothes it was not naughty to take them from the menswear department – his handyman activities more than paid for them.

He was never bored. There were always the latest televisions in stock, with endless channels and videos he could borrow. The book department had every book you could wish for. He even played computer games, although never knowing what he was supposed to be doing.

As the years went by he would sometimes think about the life he had left behind. It was another world, another country. Times change. The Englishman of the 21st Century was a vastly different animal to

Englishmen of past centuries.

With every change in his environment mankind has had to adapt and Freddy had simply adapted to the modern world. You cannot stop progress. He had seen the light and made his peace with the inevitable.

From time to time he espied Doris shopping in the store and she seemed alright. He wondered how long he had gone missing before he was missed.

Then one day Doris came accompanied by a man. Freddy took up a discreet position and had a good look at him out of curiosity. The fellow tagged along behind Doris just as he, Freddy, had done, stopping to dolefully regard anything she bought and nod in agreement at what she said.

Watching him Freddy realized that he was seeing what would have been his fate. In fact the fellow was behaving so much like the way he used to be Freddy did wonder whether Doris had even noticed he had gone missing.

They left the store and Freddy never saw them again. The rest of Freddy's life was lived as a man in perfect harmony with the world. From birth to death the store would take care of everything. All he had to do was go with the flow and not fight it.

One of the first things Freddy did after sorting out his bed and eating arrangements was to get his name on the Pickerings funeral plan. When the time duly came he was dealt with very nicely.

That year the accounts were slightly out by the cost of one funeral. But with a turnover of £100 million only Pickerings chief accountant noticed and he expertly adjusted the figures.

The Clone Conspiracies

Harry cornered Dimbleby from Bankruptcy. Dimbleby sighed; there was no escape.

"It's a great idea," enthused Harry. "There's this fellow who has fathered 53 children by 27 different women. He demands a house from the local council for each of the women who have had his children. He takes the council to the Court of Human Rights, and wins £10 million compensation for discrimination because his counsel proves he has the right to be a sex maniac. Then the council is forced to give him 27 houses, and the comedy series I have written is about the poor chap's problems in dividing his life between all 27 families.

"What do you think? A great soap, eh?"

Dimbleby was not sure. "Soaps have to be based a bit on real life."

Harry considered this for a moment. "OK, I'll make the women come from 27 different countries, and none can speak English."

Dimbleby nodded. "Yeah, that sounds believable."

Thomas Clermont walked past a great crowd of onlookers, so numerous they had to be kept in check by rows of police with linked arms. Royalty itself could hardly expect greater attention. From every vantage point television crews from around the world aimed their cameras at him. Shamelessly he presented his profile so they got good shots. He had waited a long time for success like this and it felt good. This was his chance for fame and fortune.

There is one quality a barrister must have above all others - even a talent for acting sincerely is not as important - and that is presence; courtroom charisma. Truth and innocence are no match for a booming voice and a rakish wig. The wrongdoings of rogues, the lies of liars, the swindles of swines and the piffling problems of nasty neighbours would all be plainly seen as felonies, falsehoods, fiddles and foolishness were it not for a bewigged barrister.

Such theatricality was sorely needed in Court Number Two at the Old Bailey that morning. Clermont knew this was his day, and he dug deep into his reserves of barristerial bombast.

He began in the manner of someone explaining away a simple problem. They only had to listen to him, and it would all be solved by the coffee break.

"My Lord, my client Ronald Hall pleads not guilty to the charge of the murder of Gerry Hall. He does not dispute the facts of the case, that Mr Hall died at his - my client Mr Ronald Hall's - hands when Mr Gerry Hall tried to eat my client Mr Ronald Hall. It was deliberate, not an accident, but his defence is that it was neither murder nor manslaughter.

"The circumstances leading up to Mr Hall's death were that Mr Hall had, for some time prior to the incident which led to my client being charged with murder, persistently tried to claim my client's possessions as his own. He frequently had to be ejected from my client's home and even, bizarrely behaved as though my client's wife was his - Gerry Hall's - wife.

"And the justification, which was not justification at all, that Mr Hall always put forward for his astonishing behaviour, was that he was my client.

"No attempts by the police to curtail his behaviour worked, and a legal move by my client - brought through sheer despair - to have Mr Hall put into a secure institution was unsuccessful. That was not surprising, as the deceased was not mentally disturbed. He was a perfectly sane, perfectly compos mentis but not, and this is the point, perfectly normal.

"And that, my lord, brings me to the nub of our defence. For Gerry Hall was a clone of my client. And as such he - Gerry Hall - claimed he was my client Ronald Hall.

"The tragedy began some 25 years previously, when a certain Egyptian doctor, a so-called expert on genetics, cloned my client for his parents who had wanted another son like my client who was a lovable and gifted child. At that time an impending tragedy was that this gifted and much-loved child was to die of a then incurable disease. The clone was able to provide a stem cell that saved the gifted child's life, so both grew to adulthood. Sadly the clone, although a carbon copy of his brother, was neither gifted nor lovable, lacking what might be termed 'human-ness'.

"However, for better or worse the clone existed and in this case it was for the worse. My Lord may remember the furore that followed that cloning, and subsequent clonings, with every religious, ethical and political organisation in the world having a different opinion.

"Then cloning was banned in Britain, although of course it is still a common - although illegal - practice, and there are many illicit practitioners in other parts of the world.

"That would have been that, had Mr Hall turned out to have been a successful person - to avoid using 'clone' or 'human being' as this has also been the subject of much impassioned argument.

"But he did not and Mr Hall grew up to be a curious neutral being. 'Lifeless' a person of 'no personality' 'robot-like' and 'just empty' are words that have been used to describe him. As he grew into adulthood it seems that his only reason for existing was to become my client.

"And self-evidently, he could not do so. Two into one will not go. Indeed in this case one into one would not go.

"Things came to a head when Mr Gerry Hall tried to eat my client, in the bizarre belief that by doing so he would become my client.

"One further aspect of this remarkable affair is that, for reasons best explained by Parliament, or the Church, or those civil rights people who have such strong views on so many things but not such strong resolve in shouldering responsibility for them, no legal definition as to what a clone is has ever been made.

"So, it could be argued, no legal person has been killed.

"However, that will not be the basis of my client's defence which will simply be this: He and the deceased were technically the same person.

"Therefore my client will argue that he has committed suicide - and half succeeded.

"He therefore cannot be guilty of murder."

Thereupon Clermont sat down, about to become the most famous barrister of the century. With a thunder of feet the packed Press gallery emptied of reporters dashing to file their stories.

The exodus by the Press meant that none of them saw the jury being led out by court ushers, each looking totally dazed after listening to such a mind-numbing argument.

Nevertheless they had to come to a verdict and, once their wits had found their way back from being lost in Clermont's verbal labyrinth, they did the easiest thing and found the defendant not guilty, although not guilty of what exactly probably none of them had worked out.

It was a case that was to make Clermont both famous and wealthy.

Photographers jostled to get a picture of him with his wife outside the courtroom.

"Smile! Mrs Clermont!" they urged, but to no avail. It was not until the next time she was in the news that they might have guessed why she had not smiled. Even then she was thinking of how to kill the man with his husbandly arm around her.

Slowly and painfully seemed a good way.

First seeing off his wife in a taxi Clermont walked back to his chambers in Temple Bar. His mobile rang and he saw it was Lola calling. Finding a secluded place he answered.

"So proud of you darling," she gushed. "We must have dinner to celebrate."

"Cicero's," he answered grandly. "I'll call you back darling when I've booked a table."

His mad passion for the £uscious and £avish Lola had put him thousands of pounds in debt, and the firm's accounts would not bear close scrutiny. Now, in the coming weeks he hoped his fortunes would change, and the book he had written would be hot stuff.

His new-found fame would ensure the book sold well.

Clone stories had been in the news before, but following the Hall clone case that had been reported world-wide they now appeared almost daily, fashion being what it is in the media as everywhere else.

Currently the papers were carrying reports about the South American clone armies being bred for drug warlords. They were used to fight the military forces that were trying to stop drug trafficking. Scientists employed by the drug barons had developed a fast-grow cloning technique that produced a full-sized gunman on secret cloning farms in five years. They were killed in their thousands by the government forces but they were replaced immediately from the cloning farms.

All these stories were inspiration to Harry Parsons in accounts, who spent every spare moment dreaming up ideas for films and television. He regularly sent them to the BBC and Hollywood, hoping one day to write a block-buster. Following the fashion of the moment his stories featured clones and mad scientists.

Enthusiastically he cornered Smithy in Wills about this latest brainwave.

"It's a modern version of King Kong," he enthused. "It will make me a million!"

"Well, don't tell everyone about it, they'll pinch your idea."

"Don't worry, I have had it copyrighted. It's about a clone that is developed in some back street laboratory in South America by a mad scientist that grows into a super-size man. The government decides that it cannot be allowed to survive in case it reproduces itself and the world is not big enough to take one over-sized clone let alone millions. He grows to 100 feet high.

"A lawyer - an American of course - is hired by a fringe religious group to give it the legal right to marry and have giant clone children. The lawyer is a woman and she falls in love with the giant. Mobs riot in protest for and against the clone having the right to have huge children. Millions of people get killed in the riots.

"Then he is captured by terrorists who inject him with a drug to drive him fighting mad and send him to knock down New York City. The Army and Air Force are restricted in how to fight it because of the population trapped in the carnage.

"The giant smashes the building in which the lawyer has her office and he finds her body in the wreckage. Heartbroken - because he loves her - he dies of grief. Great stuff, eh?"

"Sounds good," agreed Smithy, who was only half listening as he was more interested in the case he was immersed in right then of the clone woman suing the clone she was cloned from for maintenance for her clone children. The clone 'father' argued that it was the scientist who cloned the children who was responsible for their maintenance and the case was going to the House of Lords for a judgement.

"Yeah, sounds very good Harry. Hope it makes you that million."

"Here's another," said Harry, but Smithy escaped because Archie from Contracts came along.

So Harry buttonholed him instead. "A mad scientist - they are always mad - clones a clone. The problem is the two clones do everything as one, they talk in unison, think in unison, move in unison. They sue him for the cost of having to have everything twice in their house - two loos side by side, etc. They also sue for damages because the scientist did not clone a double woman for them to marry. You see, as they have to do everything in unison they have to have two…"

"Hollywood will pay you a million for that Harry," Archie interrupted quickly. "I'll do the contract for you - special rates for nutters."

"Thanks Archie."

The newspapers that week carried the story of police in Oklahoma who were mounting a siege on a new religious order where the cult leader had secretly made 5,000 clones of himself. He was demanding that he had the right under the Constitution to replicate himself as often as he liked. The courts had ordered the seizure of his laboratory equipment, but when they did there would still be the problem of what to do with 5,000 copies of the same maniac.

That gave Harry another great idea, and he treated Smithy again to the world premiere.

"This chap develops a clone football team, eleven players who think as one and are unbeatable. They play such perfect football they take over the league. It is a disaster for human teams. Then along comes a mysterious man who brings back all the great players when they were young. He recreates a young Pele, Maradona, Bobby Charlton, George Best, Stanley Matthews, Tom Finney, Gordon Banks - all the greats, and they challenge the clone team. Everyone in the world needs to have the human team win to restore faith in humankind, and it goes right to the final kick of the match."

"Who wins?" asked Smith.

"Don't know yet. I'm working on it. Anyway I don't want to spoil the ending for you."

Clara Clermont had decided on murdering her husband the week before his famous court victory. She had called into her husband's office to give him the house keys. He had forgotten to take them and she was going to be out when he arrived home that evening.

He had not been in the office and she left the keys with his secretary. By then it was mid-morning, time for some refreshment. Nearby were the Pacific Rooms, where they had sometimes gone in the old days, and just curious as to what it was like now, she went in for a coffee.

Nothing had changed, and the potted palms still shielded the table where they used to sit. Then she stopped and stared. That was the moment when the clock started ticking to murder. Through the palm leaves her gaze had alighted on her husband. He was with an exotic woman, holding her hands across the table and talking earnestly. The woman looked upset and he appeared to be anxiously placating her.

With the shelter of the potted palms Clara was able to get close enough to overhear their conversation, and what she heard sealed her husband's fate.

"It's all in hand darling," Clermont was telling the woman. "We'll be together soon. I'll take care of things. Just be patient."

"But she can make trouble. She'll fight over the money."

Clermont interrupted. "Don't worry, we'll have everything. Trust me. I'll take care of things."

"But will she agree to a divorce?"

"No, but that won't be a problem. Trust me, I'll take care of things."

Clermont raised the woman's left hand and touched a glittering diamond ring she was wearing.

"Do you like it darling?"

"Oh, yes, thank you darling. It's beautiful. It must have cost you a fortune, thank you. Darling, you are so good to me," she simpered.

Clara saw enough of the ring to know that a fortune was exactly what it had cost, and she choked with fury.

They prepared to leave and Clara moved to hide behind a bigger palm. As Clermont and his lover left he paused close to the palm to kiss her goodbye.

"Don't worry," he assured the woman again. "She won't be a problem."

And in so saying, neither would he.

Clara Clermont had left the café with her mind made up. Her marriage had been tottering for a while now. She had long guessed there was someone else. But it was not that - she herself had a lover - it was the 'she won't be a problem' and 'I'll take care of things'.

There was no mistaking what he meant. So as she made her way back home all she was thinking about now was how to take care of *him*, and *that* was not going to be a problem.

She telephoned her lover Chris Forrest. He was always a comfort when she needed a shoulder to cry on. Until now she had never quite summoned up the resolve to do as he wanted and leave her husband. She had met Chris through the legal social circles in which he and her husband moved. She was worried about getting her share of the matrimonial money even though Chris, who was a specialist in matrimony law, always assured her that he would get her a good settlement.

Now she was going for the lot after hearing her husband's plans for dealing with her.

'I'm not stupid,' fumed Clara to herself. 'It is plain what they are planning - they want me out of the way and there is only one way they can do that. Well, two can play at the murder game!'

That evening Clermont poured himself and Clara a glass of wine after dinner, and toasted his success.

"By the way, dear," he said. "Better be careful not to let the media know about us having house clones, eh?"

Clara knew what he meant. Following her husband's celebrated defence of Hall, the fact that the defence barrister and his wife had been cloned would make uncomfortable headlines.

She had always regretted that they had had themselves cloned. At the time it had been all the rage. Finding home help had been a nightmare and cloning had been the answer for many affluent families.

They had had fast-grow clones that seemed perfectly satisfactory as butler and housekeeper, but Clara had never been comfortable with them. They way they looked at you, even when they smiled, as though they wanted to ... but she could not put it into words. Just 'ugh!' Once she had caught the housekeeper clone trying on her clothes. Seeing her dressed like that had been like looking at herself and it had been eerie.

Dutifully she raised her glass to the toast. Looking at the amber liquid the way to kill him was suddenly simple.

He liked his evening tot before bed.

Harry nobbled Angie in Conveyancing in the tea break to tell her about his script for a blockbuster.

"It's about clones who try to take over the world and destroy all human life," he enthused.

"People shouldn't mess around with nature," said Angie. "Remember those nutty Aussies way back in 2000 and something. They found a way to kill off the so-called 'fat gene' in overweight people. They could - and did - eat as much as they liked without getting fat. The only trouble they got hot instead. Before anyone realised how hot, millions of people had had the fat gene eradicated and they hot hotter and hotter. Nobody could do anything about it and they ended up all being cooked. It was terrible."

"The trouble is," said Clermont who was passing by and overheard her, "scientists seem to forget Einstein's theory when they start something."

He could see from Angie's expression that she did not catch on to what he meant, but he did not explain. He liked being clever.

After the famous clone murder case Clermont's law practice was soon Midas rich. Life was hectic, as his book The Talking Head was selling very well. Soon he would have a villa in Spain and a farmhouse in the Dordogne and living with £uscious £ola.

There was just the matter of Mrs Clermont, who would want half his money, and Clermont knew he would need plenty to keep the sexy and expensive Lola in his bed. A couple of million was peanuts these days.

By now their affair and the rift simmering between the Clermonts was common gossip throughout Temple Bar, but as is often the case, those who were gossiped about were deaf.

Clermont took a week off from the office to promote his book. His agent picked him up and took him to his fifth media interview that day. Tonight he was on the Dick and Diana Teatime Talk in another of a furious round of interviews publicising The Talking Head.

"Let's begin at the beginning," said Dick. "This man walked into your office one morning, and then what happened? What did he say?"

Clermont had been well schooled by a leading public relations outfit and held up his book, so that viewers would get a good look at the title.

"There was also the extraordinary affair of The Blob."

"Ah yes," said Clermont taking the opportunity again to hold up the book in front of the camera, "and that's all in here as well."

"Tell us first about The Talking Head," urged Diana.

"Yes. Well, it all began when a man called into my office and after hearing his extraordinary story I went with him to his flat, and there was The Talking Head. I was absolutely astounded. The head was being kept on a platter, and the story that they both told me - because the head was a perfectly normal, intelligent, human head but simply without a body - was that it was an experiment that had gone wrong.

"The man, who had called me was The Talking Head's friend and had rescued him from a laboratory where he was being kept for more experiments. I was able through a court order to have the head recognised as a legal human being."

"At great cost, as many people have pointed out. You were paid £2 million in legal aid fees," said Dick.

Clermont responded to that smoothly. "But here was a human being, and was legally entitled to live as one. What price can you put on life?"

Diana changed the subject: "Well, no doubt we will get plenty of reaction, but now tell us about The Blob."

"Yes, The Blob. Well, a similar scenario, except it is not a head, just a blob and cannot speak. Although many people claim to be able to communicate with it telepathically. More and more people are becoming interested, and again my law practice has also been instrumental in obtaining the right for The Blob to be treated as a living creature."

The next day's newspapers reported The Blob's followers had constructed a bullet-proof glass building in which to house it. Now it was on display to thousands who queued from dawn to dusk to file past, and many swore that they could communicate with it.

Like wildfire a cult was growing round The Blob, and people claimed that It was guiding them through their personal troubles. Also foremost in the news was the rapid progress of the career of The Talking Head, who had just been signed up to present his own television show.

Harry was eager to tell whoever would listen about the twist he was adding to his clone football team saga. It was Fred the cleaner's turn this time.

"It's a great idea," said Harry. "Without any of the famous players realising it, the scientist had acquired bits of them - snips of hair that their hairdressers sold to fans as souvenirs, and so on. I'll work out how he does it later, and he uses the bits to clone carbon copies of them. So they are faced with having to play themselves! Get it? They have to win to preserve their identity and stop clones being thought of better than them."

When Harry finished, Fred was speechless.

"I knew you'd be impressed," grinned Harry.

Clermont's staff were becoming overloaded with work now the practice had received so much publicity. Egos were getting tetchy at the morning meeting to apportion briefs.

Harold the senior solicitor handed a brief to Hunter, who unenthusiastically asked: "What's this?"

"A man claims damages from his local authority for allowing two homosexuals to adopt him way back in the beginning of the century. Claims he has suffered trauma not being raised in a conventional family."

"What's a conventional family these days, for God's sake?"

"Who knows, but he should get half a million. No one will be able to prove he hasn't been traumatised. Hire the usual psychiatrists."

"Why can't Nikes take it on?"

"Nikes has a full caseload. The chimpanzee case is enough in itself."

"The what?"

"The chimpanzee case. Some scientist fellow has mated with a chimp and produced, with the aid of some scientific jiggery-pokery, a family of human chimps."

"Good God! Human chimps? What on Earth…?"

"He is seeking to have them recognized as human beings. It will be quite a sensation when the Press get hold of it."

"Yeah, I bet. What are you working on now - shouldn't you be at court on that harassed woman case?"

"That finished this morning."

"What happened? Did you win?"

"Of course. Don't we always - even if we lose!" He smirked.

"It baffles me why these women in harassment at work cases take that sort of behaviour from men," said a young clerk, new to the office. "She endured two years of her boobs being grabbed, insulted about her big bum, rubbed up against in the lift, sexist jokes. Surely no normal woman would stand that for one minute. And she was married - what was her husband doing about it, eh? She must be a fool! Why on earth did she put up with for so long?"

"That's why."

Seeing the young clerk's blank expression the senior lawyer waved the court papers under his nose.

"£200,000, that's why. She kept a detailed diary. She's no fool. The boss was the fool."

The penny dropped. "Ah, I see."

"You have got a lot to learn about the legal game, young man."

Harry lined up beside Clermont in the men's loo and, a captive audience for the duration of a pee, Clermont had to listen to another of Harry's plots.

"It's about a man who gets himself cloned and sends the clone out to rob banks and things like that, but always making sure at the same time he has a cast-iron alibi as to where he is, and that it is always a long away from the scene of the robbery.

"The police finally catch the man's clone, but cannot prove it was anything to do with the original, and the man simply abandons the clone which is now of no use. The clone is sent to prison, and when he comes out he avenges himself by killing the original and taking his place.

"What do you think Tom? Great stuff, eh?"

"Great story, Harry. I suppose you never know how clever clones might be."

As he was to find out.

Clermont's butler clone helped him on with his overcoat as he prepared to leave for the office. As he brushed his boss's shoulders the clone again felt the surge of emotion that he had come to realise from studying humans was jealousy. The feeling pleased him. He wanted to be human. Watching his master walk down the garden path towards his Mercedes he again found himself thinking of how easy it would be to become one.

So very easy.

He turned, and almost bumped into Mrs Clermont. Their eyes met, and he saw the cold dislike in hers. She never felt at ease when she was near her husband's clone. She shivered as the clone went back to his duties.

Harry had another great idea, which he had sent off to the BBC for a programme. He nailed Smithy in the corridor to tell him all about it, with his customary enthusiasm. "Did you know that 99 per cent of a chimpanzee's genes are the same as yours?"

"Really," said Smithy, ready to see the cheeky young bugger off with a flea in his ear. "And why mine, may I ask? Yours, I would imagine are 99.99 per cent."

"No, no, no! Everybody's. Everybody's genes are mostly the same as the chimps. That's what gave me this great idea for a film. A scientist tries to mix up human and chimps genes to make an intelligent chimp..."

"...or a bloody ugly human..."

"....yeah, right, but what he does is create a giant chimp, which is like King Kong. At the same time the rival scientist I told you about in my other idea has created the giant clone. They have to battle it out for supremacy, while at the same time the world's armies are trying to kill them and stop the scientists making more copies. Great stuff, eh?"

"Excuse me, I need a cup of tea."

Just exactly how to murder his wife continued to preoccupy Clermont. He had been wearing his brain out thinking up complicated schemes. Then a solution presented itself in one of the court cases someone in the office was dealing with. Not very interesting, so the job had been given to a junior lawyer. It was run of the mill case of a householder charged with murder after waking up to be confronted with a burglar and killing him in a struggle.

Clermont smiled as he realised there was no need for anything complicated. No cunning plan or false alibi, which as a barrister he had seen all too often entrap murderers in a web of their own making. Keep it simple. He would just kill her, and blame a burglar. No one would ever suspect him.

Enough thinking about it. Let's get on with it.

Chris Forrest was feeling pressured. Money, money, money! Another bad run at the tables last night. He needed Clara to make up her mind to leave Clermont. She would able to take half his money with her. He would see to that - financial litigations in separations and divorces were his legal speciality.

He met her for a discreet lunch and gently but skillfully left her with the impression that unless she made up her mind, well, he had a life to lead. It can't go on like this, it was breaking his heart.

He was not a barrister for nothing. He could have played the Old Vic as any sly villain in literature.

So Clara decided. It was now or never.

It was all carefully planned. First Clermont made sure that the back door was unlocked and wedged open. He checked his watch. Coronation Street had been on for ten minutes.

By chance, at the same time the clone housekeeper set about tidying the drawing room. Lying on the settee was Mrs Clermont's new coat. Like the clone butler she fantasised about being a real human. She put the coat on, and posed before a mirror. Delighted, she smiled at her reflection; she looked exactly like Mrs Clermont.

Clermont made a final check that the back door, which could not be opened from the outside, was open. He had arranged it to look as though it had been prevented from closing properly by a loose rug. Then he picked up the steel bar and made his way to the drawing room where he expected his wife to be watching Coronation Street as usual.

Clara had the poisoned whisky bottle ready. Her mind was racing, and she had forgotten Coronation Street. She could plant the bottle any time, but she was getting anxious. Having the poisoned bottle made her nervous. The sooner she swapped the bottles the better.

She had checked the day before on the bottle in the drinks cabinet in his den and then emptied the poisoned bottle to about the same level. He only had one or two measures each night, so it would not have altered much. All she needed was an opportunity to replace it when he was out of his den.

On impulse, as it seemed quiet in the house, she went out into the garden to look through the den window. It was lucky timing as she saw him leaving the room, wearing his coat so he must be going out.

Why not now? She was ready. Her plan had ingrained itself deeply in her mind and suddenly she decided. The door was open and her legs just took her into his den. Fighting rising panic she made the switch and hurried out, accidentally kicking the loose rug out of the way, so allowing the self locking door to close.

Then she walked around the outside of house and got into her car. She called her friend Annette and suggested they met and had a chat and a drink.

It would give her time to calm down.

Holding the steel bar in gloved hands Clermont opened the drawing room door. Seeing the familiar coat for a split second his nerve wavered. Panic threatened his resolve and at the same moment she started to turn. She would see him and scream and…...he delivered the first blow, then another and another. Then he threw the bar onto the settee. Not bearing to look at the body he made his way out of the front door to his car and quickly drove to his golf club, making sure he was seen on arrival. The timing would be alibi enough, although there would be no reason to suspect him.

Two police cars were outside, and an officer was guarding the door when Mrs Clermont arrived back home.

"What's happened?" she demanded.

The policeman had been told there was a maid and, assuming it was her, he answered: "Your mistress Mrs Clermont has been murdered by an intruder."

"My mistress! What on earth do you mean? That's impossible! I'm…."

"I'm afraid it is the truth."

It was only the numbing effect shock can have on people that stopped her saying any more. Looking through door as the police carried out their investigation she saw her coat on her clone, and realised what had prompted their presumption. She stayed silent, needing time to think.

The poison bottle! She still had not disposed of it, and any moment he could have a drink - in fact in this stressful time he was very likely to have one.

But she was refused permission to touch anything in the house and had to stay at a friend's for the night. Luckily Clermont had been taken straight down to the police station to help with their investigation, and that would give her a chance to return tomorrow and get rid of the bottle. Murdering him would have to wait until another day.

But Clermont returned from the police station just after midnight and by then he was allowed into his study. He needed that drink now!

The clone butler heard his cry and the thud of him falling. Hurrying into the room he tripped over Clermont's body.

He turned on the light and then sat down to slowly take in the scene - the opened bottle, the spilled glass by the body, the face contorted in agony, hands grasping the stomach. Having secretly overheard Mrs Clermont talking to Chris Forrest on the telephone and knowing the situation between them he slowly but certainly came to work it all out.

It was his chance to become a human. He took the poisoned whisky bottle and planted it in Mrs Clermont's room.

Then he carefully dressed the corpse in his butler clothes.

When the police told her that the butler had also been murdered Clara Clermont was struck dumb with shock for the second time. Then she saw the butler dressed in her husband's clothes and realised it was not Clermont. It was those eyes that gave the clone away: cold and inhuman.

Clara's dilemma was that if she could not prove she was herself, then she would not be able to claim the money. But if she did prove it, then she became the prime suspect for her husband's murder. Desperate, she called Forrest.

Forrest was worried. There had been panic in Clara's voice when she called, imploring him to meet her right away. When he heard her story, he knew he had to do something quickly.

"Don't worry," he told her, "I'll think of something."

It took him a minute. If Clara could not prove she was not her clone, she would not be able to claim the money, or if she could it would take years. Forrest had been getting tired of things even before this happened, and now he had lost interest altogether. No money, and all the bad publicity that would come of being involved, as the 'other man'. Worse, perhaps suspicion would fall on him!

They would never able to prove anything - and of course he would be able to charge for interviews. Could get some big media fees. Tempting, but no, he wanted out.

"Next time Mrs Clermont calls me, refer her to McAllister in the murder team," he told his secretary.

As it happens that was all academic, as with their usual plodding thoroughness the police found the poison bottle in hidden in Clara's room. Then they discovered that the door through which any intruder would have had to use to get into the den had been locked and could not have been opened from the outside. They learned from Clermont's colleagues of his affair with Lola and the strain between the Clermonts.

"Clermont killed his wife, and then he drank the poison that she had already left for him," said the Inspector. "If that is what happened, she got her revenge from the grave."

"But how do we know it was not the clones who did it, knowing that the Clermont's hated each other and would get the blame?" said the sergeant.

"We don't," replied his boss. "That's why the prosecutor's office has ordered us to do it this way. I have been practising to get it right."

With that the two made their way back to the Clermont house.

The Inspector confronted Clara and the butler clone and cautioned them both. Then he took a deep breath and proceeded to make legal history.

"Clara Clermont or Clara Clermont's clone I am arresting you both for the murders of Clara Clermont and or Clara Clermont's clone. I am also arresting you both for the murders of yourselves and each other and for the two dead bodies whoever they are.

"Thomas Clermont or Thomas Clermont's clone I am arresting you both for the murders of Thomas Clermont and or Thomas Clermont's clone. I am also arresting both of you for the murders of yourselves and each other and the two dead bodies whoever they are."

As the bewildered pair were led away the Inspector was badly in need of a cup of tea. Shaking his head world-wearily as he watched the sergeant typing up the report he mused: "How do people manage to make a mess of everything they do? Top creatures on the planet and they couldn't organise a booze-up in a brewery. Why do they make their lives so bloody complicated?"

"Dunno Sir. Perhaps that's what comes of being clever."

The Inspector lowered his voice and glanced behind to make sure no one heard:"Listen and learn sergeant.When we take over the world, if we want to survive, we must remember not to be too clever."

The Man Who Squashed the World

Charlie Barnes lay on his back looking up into a blue sky and dreamily watched little white clouds scudding. Sometimes they were going from left to right, sometimes from right to left, then slantwise, according to which way the boat swung on its moorings. From where he lay on the deck this was all Charlie could see, and it was as though he was serenely floating in space.

This was the life! Not a care in the world.

That was nice, as he had had enough of the cares of the world lately. He was a simple fellow: work, pretty girls, holidays, a few beers. All this stuff about global warming, glaciers melting, holes in the ozone. Like those little white clouds, it was all over his head.

Important stuff of course; very worrying if you kept thinking about it. He tried not to think about it, but it was difficult with Jeremy around.

All Charlie had to do was keep an eye on the drilling equipment on the boat which was moored five miles off the Hampshire coast.

It was the sort of job that just suited Charlie. Good pay and no worries. Charlie was not one for worrying. Not like Jeremy, his boss on the boat. Jeremy seemed to do enough worrying for the human race. Even now Charlie could hear him talking on the telephone to his scientist mates ashore, and as always the conversation was about ozone layers, temperatures, sea levels and the weather.

No, Charlie was not one for worrying. Anyway, he would much rather be thinking about Lisa. Charlie had met her last time he was ashore - or rather had set eyes on her but had not yet actually got round to making a date. Well, she was busy serving behind the bar and the place was crowded. Charlie had treated her to his best chat-up lines and there was no mistaking that look in her eye. He could not wait for the next time he could take the dingy ashore.

No, if you had your priorities set right there was nothing wrong with the world. Nothing that a pint and pie wouldn't cure. And Lisa.

Until shore leave he was content just to be lying here gazing up into a beautiful blue yonder. Today, at any rate, the ozone layer seemed to be functioning OK.

Yes, Charlie was easy-going. Easy-going to a fault sometimes, as more than once since he had signed aboard the good ship Driller - an old barge really - Jeremy had had to rouse him from slumber.

"Wake up Charlie, wake up!"

Charlie had always been partial to an after-lunch nap.

There was only himself and Jeremy on board. That was all the crew that was needed, once the drilling had started. Charlie just sat around all day and kept an eye on the instruments and made sure the boat was in position over the hole it was drilling.

Lots of clever stuff seemed to be going on what with banks of computers on board and Jeremy forever talking on the phone to the company head office on-shore. From bits he overheard it seemed to Charlie that Jeremy expected the world to end any minute!

Mind you, Charlie thought Jeremy was an interesting fellow. He certainly knew a lot about global warming and important stuff like that. Astronomy too, and at night he would spend hours looking at the stars through a telescope installed on board as part of the ship's scientific equipment.

He would let Charlie have a look sometimes, and he had to admit seeing that immense array of shining stars did make a man think a bit deeper than he would over a pie and pint.

Having finished his telephone conversation Jeremy was now poring over some scientific papers. In an attempt to show a bit of interest Charlie hoisted himself on one elbow and looked across at him.

"You worry a lot about the weather and pollution and such, don't you."

"It's a big concern. We are messing things up a bit."

"We've got to have fires to keep warm, cars to move around in. We can't all go by bike. Do you reckon there's anything we can do about it then? Are we all done for?"

Jeremy smiled. "Not everyone, with a bit of luck."

Charlie laughed. "So is this what we're doing on this boat then? Saving the world?"

"You think you can save the world Charlie? Better hurry. Time's running out."

"Yeah? What's drilling into the seabed got to do with saving the world?" Charlie was beginning to get curious, despite himself.

"This is just a bit of what we are doing. Earth samples, air samples, oh, there are many aspects of our research."

"And all this gazing at the Moon through that telescope, what's that got to do with saving the world?"

"Not saving, escaping," said Jeremy.

"Escaping? Escaping to where?"

Jeremy clammed up. "Never mind, Charlie. It's over your head."

"What, the Moon?" Charlie's little joke was not that funny but it made Jeremy laugh.

Sometimes a bunch of other eggheads would come aboard to talk in riddles with Jeremy but usually he went ashore for meetings, which he was about to do today.

"It's all set up," he told Charlie. "The computers have been set. All you've got to do is watch the instruments. You know what to do."

"Leave it to me," said Charlie.

"See you in a couple of days," said Jeremy and set off for the shore in the dinghy.

All in order and everything thought of - except Charlie's penchant for a nap. Nothing nicer than settling down on a boat drifting gently on a calm sunny sea. Nothing nicer...hmmm...zzzz.

Then crash! Charlie woke in alarm, and this time it was not the sky he was gazing at but the deck, then the sky, then the deck again. The sky was whirling madly round and round as the boat swung on its anchor. Charlie tried to stand up. He caught a glimpse of the sea swirling round the boat like a giant whirlpool. Everything was spinning and then the boat lurched violently and he was sent flying across the deck.

Whack! He hit his head on something hard and was knocked out cold.

When Charlie came round he lay on his back for a long while gathering his wits. Slowly he got to his feet and then realised he was no longer on the boat. He was standing on a high shingle beach and his clothes were soaking wet. The boat? He must have fallen overboard and somehow got washed up on the beach. He looked out to sea for any sign of the boat and - where was the sea? As far as he could see there were just mudflats and rocks sloping down into the distance.

The sea had disappeared.

"You've come round then?"

Startled, Charlie looked round and saw a man standing nearby. There was no one else around, just him and Charlie. The man was grey-haired with a goatee beard and a studious look about him. After asking his question, he did not seem interested in the answer and turned and stood gazing seawards - or more accurately mudwards.

Then he seemed to remember his manners. "Hello, I'm Professor Solvit."

Polite introductions in the circumstances were odd but Charlie told him his name, then asked: "What happened?"

The professor indicated the wilderness of mud in front of them. "That happened."

"What?"

"Someone drilled a blessed great hole in the seabed, and that happened."

This was all too much for Charlie to take in, and he just stood there completely bewildered.

"The sea must have fallen 200 300 metres." The professor seemed more impressed by this than alarmed for the world's fate.

"What happened?" Charlie finally asked again. "Who are you? How did I get here?"

"I'm a scientist at the environmental research station up there." He indicated a building on a hill. "My colleagues and I found you down there in the mud. Pulled you up here to dry out."

Charlie had a headache. This was all too much.

"What happened? A hole?"

"A drilling boat out in the bay. Some fool drilled a hole in the earth's crust. It caved in and half the oceans ran down it."

Some fool - Charlie gathered his senses enough to admit nothing.

"What does that mean," he asked.

"Oh, it's shrunk the world. The oceans have run into the Earth's interior, somehow making the Earth implode, wrinkle in effect, with mountains higher and seas deeper. Luckily not that much sea ran away, it's more a case of the ocean floors being much deeper. Otherwise we would have serious problems with the hot larva at the earth's core."

All the while he was talking the professor gazing into the ether, really more concerned with his thoughts.

"I had a mate with me," said Charlie.

"That would be Jeremy," said the professor.

"Yes! You know him?"

"Jeremy? Yes, bright fellow Jeremy. World expert on the environment."

"What's happened to him?"

The professor simply pointed up into the sky.

Heaven? "Dead!" cried Charlie.

"No, no. He and his colleagues are on the Moon."

Charlie stared at the scientist. On the Moon? The man was barmy. Charlie rubbed his aching head.

"I must be dreaming," he said.

The professor regarded Charlie wisely. "As Shakespeare said, it's all a dream."

Continuing his thoughtful monologue he went on: "We thought they were up to something." The scientist was talking more to himself than Charlie. "Very clever. Risky, but it might just work.

"They realised that the world was heading for disaster. So they planned an escape with a spaceship - bought one second-hand from Cape Canaveral, so I heard.

"They intend to build a city up there and are taking up water and air from the earth in tubes." He pointed to the sky. "Look, you can see."

Charlie looked, and saw what appeared to be a giant hosepipe spiralling up into the blue.

"That's the tube that's sucking up the water." The scientist shook his head sceptically. "I don't know whether it will work."

Charlie thought about all this for a while, then remembered from his school lessons that the Moon did not spin round and got extremely hot on one side

"The water will all boil away up there," he said.

"From some data that they left behind we think they plan to build a line of giant rockets to start the Moon revolving.

"With the air and water from the earth they think that a weather system will develop in which humans can live. Very ambitious."

Charlie's poor brain was whirling but he tried to make some sense of all this.

"How are they going to keep the hosepipe in the right place? The world will turn and snap it off!"

"Oh, a girdle round the earth, a sort of gyro."

"What? An enormous great strap round the world!" Charlie had to laugh.

"No! No! A computer-controlled electro-magnetic girdle that..." But the scientist could not be bothered with all this. His mind was off again into the scientific ether.

"That's a thought. We could perhaps cut it off in the stratosphere and use it to pump up ozone - or expel pollution and heat?

"Hmm....Yes, expel all the heat and pollution through tubes. With a series of tubes around the world...expelling heat and pollution into space...controlled by computers...mmm...yes, possible. Earth's temperature could be kept at the right level and the environment kept in ideal condition...yes....mmm...possible, possible.

"And rocket power - simply drill a hole to the centre of the earth, stick a rocket in it, wait for pressure to build up, and then pop! The rocket flies out into space with all our nuclear waste on board. Yes, feasible I think, with a few calculations..."

Ruminating to himself on this for a few minutes, the scientist continued, still talking more to himself than to Charlie.

"At first they will build giant habitats on the Moon, rather like the tropical gardens in that big greenhouse thing they had down in Cornwall, then they will see if air and water can be made to stick to the Moon. That was rather far-fetched I thought."

Suddenly Charlie, who had not understood a word of all this, was anxious.

"So what is going to happen to us?"

"Oh, we'll muddle through. The human race always does. We survived the Flood. No doubt we would have survived whatever killed the dinosaurs if we had been around then."

The scientist was speaking offhandedly, as though all the while thinking of things rather more interesting.

"Quite fascinating finding those lost civilisations. Some are claiming that one of them is Atlantis - could be," he ruminated.

"It was under the Aegean Sea- or where the Aegean was! Now there is - what? – half-a-dozen underground civilisations thrown up by the upheaval. There's a pygmy civilisation under Africa I hear, and an albino race revealed that was once five kilometres below Sweden. Shows there must have been quite a few cataclysmic events like this through the eons. Civilisations entombed and forced to live underground. Not cave-ins caused by some fool on a drilling rig I bet!"

Charlie kept his innocent expression firmly in place. The scientist continued his ruminating.

"Well, no more worries about global warming at least. Now we have something bigger to worry about. Come to think of it, has Man has ever solved his problems, or just caused bigger problems to worry about!"

Then he brightened up. "In fact it's a rather interesting time!"

Charlie looked down at the sea of mud that sloped down into the vast hole that was once the English Channel. 'Interesting' was not the word he had in mind. Right cock-up was more like it.

He put in a good word for 'the fool'.

"Well, at least we won't all be under water if the ice caps melt."

"Oh, that would not have been a problem. Deepening the oceans using underwater conveyor-excavators, putting the stuff on the ocean floors back on the land," the scientist replied, as though explaining the ABC to a simpleton.

"And a reservoir as standard under every new-built house to store rainwater off the roof.

"They made such a palaver of it all! Worrying about overheating the world, and never once thought of recycling all the steam from their kitchens to warm their homes. And why have houses roofed with tiles and slates? Why not glass, to make a greenhouse heated from the warmth of the inhabitants to enable them to grow at least half the food they need? I advocated this years ago!

"The heat from more and more people was creating more global warming than anything else, but they couldn't see that! If they had banned energetic sports they would have prevented all that heat from millions of sweaty bodies!

"Even the simple matter of rivers flooding - all they had to do was lay pipes from points along rivers straight into the sea to pump away floodwater before it reached towns. Or just flat pipes with floats that open it up as flood waters rise to carry it safely away. Or save it in tanks for drought periods. So simple!"

As he spoke his voice rose with exasperation at having such obtuse people in charge of things.

"And houses - why not build them floatable? Boat houses. On a retractable anchor chain so the householder can pull the house back when the floods subside? Even tidier, houses built on top of poles that sink into the ground, and go up and down with the floodwater. If there is a giant wave due to an undersea earthquake - I expect we will get a few of those until the Earth's crust settles down - they could design houses boat-shaped to ride out the wave. Not tidy, but better than traditional homes. But no, no one listens to logic!" The professor's growing head of exasperation finally blew off with a loud snort.

"Times I tried to tell them! All sorts of simple solutions. Giant freezers at the North and South poles to keep them frozen, large reservoirs to store surplus water, houses on stilts - all sorts of solutions. All sorts!

"And all that fuss when we got snow, blocked roads and such. This is an island surrounded by sea, and the sea round our island does not freeze. Seaside towns had icy roads, yet all they had to do was spray some salt water – not more than a few yards away – on the ice and, solved! The ice and snow melts. Seawater pumped along pipes to spray on main roads and motorways – how simple and obvious is that?

"And on the subject of freeze-ups and sea water – why on earth were flights grounded because of frozen runways? All they had to do was put long ski-wheels on planes. Lots of wheels – ball bearings in effect – inside a long ski. It would operate in the dry or on ice, perhaps even better on ice.

"And why not use the sea coast, cordoned off areas to slow down storms, as a place to land planes – commercial planes to start with to gain experience for passenger planes.

"Volcano dust blotting out the sun - simple, all you need are vacuum tubes held up by balloons that suck the dust down into the sea. Mess up the sea for a while, but better than an ice age!

"In fact, why suck it into the sea? Everything is of some use to someone. Volcano dust has its uses - building, chemistry." Yes, the professor looked pleased with that reasoning.

"And why bother with all those wind farms, causing all that palaver from nature lovers? Didn't they realise wind howls with gale force round every corner? Even a breeze provides power to harness. And every house has corners - and roofs. Horizontal and vertical turbines that the wind could drive both ways on roofs and corners of houses - hardly noticeable. Every large building in every city could generate its own power with turbines on the corners of the building. Chicago could supply half of America! Windy alleyways - a goldmine!

"Quaint olde worlde windmills on country cottages. All the power a household needed. In fact Dutch-style windmills look nice. Just along the coast is Portland, a high windy place stuck out to sea and exposed to the wind. Cover it with old-fashioned windmills and it would look great, a tourist attraction, and at the same time provide all the electricity Britain needs.

"And if they must have giant public windmills why not on top of mountains where no one can see them? Who would see a giant windmill on top of Everest? The winds up there would create enough electricity for the whole world!"

At this point the fuse blew again.

"They don't think! They didn't listen to commonsense! Haven't they heard of Einstein's theory? Every problem creates its solution - that's the same as every action has a reaction. Obvious! There's a downhill to every uphill, so every person going down can pull another up. One fat man can pull two thin men up. You slide down, and your slide generates the power to pull someone up. So simple! So obvious! Not everyone will want to be pulled up in, say, a hotel or shopping mall, as some will be fitness freaks who want to walk up, so it will work without any problems."

The scientist stopped, simmering quietly for a few moments, then continued in his former thinking-aloud mode.

"We were always intrigued as to what Jeremy and his colleagues were up to. They must have been planning going to the Moon eventually but this," he indicated the shrunken terrain before him, "hurried things up for them."

"Yes, but what about us!"

The scientist smiled in superior fashion.

"Survival of the fittest, as they say, and survival in the 21st Century was always going to about brains, not brawn.

"So after all perhaps the fool that caused all this has saved the world from disaster, given it a new chance. We don't have to worry about sea levels now, there is more land to be colonised and the sea that drained away seems to have settled harmlessly in underground caves and fissures."

Then another thought occurred. He waved an iffy hand this way and that as he looked up at the Moon.

"Maybe they were going to drain some of the sea away to stop the world flooding." He nodded, intrigued. "Yes, perhaps that was part of their plan. Perhaps that was why they were drilling the hole in the seabed. Then, this happened, so now there will not be enough water for both worlds. Some day, when we that are left on the Earth sort ourselves out, we might have to cut the tube. Goodness, with the world messed up like this and those on the Moon with all that expertise they have, perhaps we are in for a war of the worlds!"

Charlie looked around at the sea of mud stretching out of sight, and behind at the jumble of mountains that had once been the typical gentle rolling hills of England.

"Where have the people gone?"

"Oh, there will be survivors. Eventually there will be new races, new tribes.

"I hear that people have started to appear from civilisations that earlier disasters had left imprisoned underground. Time just stood still for them apparently. There are pygmy princes with their entourages, and gladiators and centurions, Egyptian priests and Vikings from underworld civilisations entombed thousands of years ago.

"They are fighting their old wars all over again as though nothing had changed." He paused, thinking. "Hmm, that could cause a bit of a problem."

Then he brightened again. "Still, it's happened. It's given the world a new beginning, a new chance to make a success of things. We were making a bit of a muck of it.

"There's a paradise created on the other side of the world, I hear. New mountains have enclosed a region to form a country with a perfect climate. The mountains contain a year-round weather ecology with warm rain at night, temperate sun by day and just a week-long winter with snow.

"And apparently we hear that some people have started colonising the giant holes in the Earth that were created when this happened. They say the temperature in them is always at a nice even level, plenty of fresh water, lots of waterfalls for power. Always adaptable, humans.

"Probably that's how the underground Atlantis civilisations started, with people going underground then getting sealed off.

"So, don't worry, there will be plenty of people left. New countries will form, new nations. We'll manage. We always have."

Charlie's thoughts were whirling round his head like socks in a washing machine. He looked out at the sea of mud.

"What if the sea comes flooding back?"

"A tidal wave you mean. Too far out now to matter, but in future seaside beaches could be protected by fine-mesh nets lying on the seabed that the sea-flood itself pushes up, slowing down the force, then they would operate the opposite way when the flood recedes, catching people to prevent them being washed out to sea. Rough and ready, but it will save lives."

Then an amusing thought briefly brightened the professor's countenance.

"It will catch a few fish at the same time!"

All too much for Charlie. Oh well things to be done, like surviving. Charlie, not a thinker but a do-er, got down to building a shelter and gathering food. Then he cleared some ground to plant crops, collecting corn seed from abandoned farm fields.

Like Professor Solvit said there would be survivors and new tribes forming. All Charlie had to do was find a woman and start a new tribe, just as man had always done. Then bless his soul, barely had this thought occurred when Lisa appeared.

The pub had fallen down a big hole she told him, but she had escaped. Thankfully she fell into his manly arms. There is nothing like a woman to inspire survival, and soon they had a lovely cottage and loads of kids.

Life was not too bad, and it did not seem to matter that the Earth was all wrinkled and squashed up. The terrestrial upheavals had thrown up gold and precious metals and jewels in abundance, so they became ornaments for everyone.

Old Mother Nature coped with the changed environment very quickly and they were soon growing enough food for themselves and selling the surplus to the scientists on the hill who were too busy with the mysteries of life to have time for its necessities.

People started exploring to form new countries. So they started a wayside pub to give them food and shelter as they passed by on their travels. Lisa became a barmaid again and Charlie was mine host.

Sometimes when having a nap after lunch he would dream of Jeremy and hear him calling.

"Come on Charlie wake up, this won't do!"

Charlie would wake up, gaze up at the tube to the Moon, and wonder what Jeremy was doing stuck up there. Even a squashed-up world was a more interesting place to live on than the Moon. Then he would think that perhaps being clever was not all that it was cracked up to be.

After all, Jeremy, it was me who saved the world from global warming!

A Horse Called Harry

Tommy was all for telling the Press. Whenever a punter makes a killing, especially with an accumulator, the big bookmakers are happy to let the world know they have been stung for half a million or so.

It stimulates trade and bookies know, just as well as punters, that it is not going to happen very often. For every bad day for bookmakers there's a month of bad days for hopeful Joe Punter. That's what? 30-1?

True, Rolls Bookmakers phone account customer Mr John Williams had not won half a million, only five grand on a treble and that was hardly the stuff to make a story. Winning £5,000 is nice, but you don't give up the day job. The story was in how it and other similar bets of his had been won.

But the boss Vic Rolls said no, we'll keep this to ourselves.

Office manager Tommy did not understand this caution.

"Why, you don't suspect anything fishy do you? The fellow just likes doing special names. We'll take those sorts of bets all day."

Tommy was right, if every punter bet like Williams, on coincidences, family names and so on, bookmakers would be even richer. There would be the occasional big win - always capped by their pay-out limit - but day after day bookmakers would need a removal van to take their money to the bank.

Vic winked at Tommy. "This fellow has won a few bob lately backing horses with Harry in their name. Usually tenner doubles, sometimes a treble. He is on a roll, just a lucky punter. While he's on a roll, while his luck lasts, we can off-load his bets. If they lose, then all we lose is £20 or so. But if he stays lucky, we get lucky."

Vic was not bothered about the money. A couple of grand here or there is nothing to a bookmaker. It was the craic, as the Irish say. Sometimes being a bookmaker was a bit too much like being an accountant. This would be a diversion in the routine business of becoming wealthy.

Bookmakers have the unsporting habit of refusing bets from punters who are too lucky, but despite his wins this punter looked to be no serious threat. Even so, Vic had Williams checked out and discovered intriguingly that he was a stable lad and work jockey at Freddie Moon's yard at Chantry, where 30 per cent of England's racehorses are trained.

Bets that come from training sources are scrutinized by bookies, but they are invariably single bets, relying on inside information.

Evidently our Mr Williams was just one of those punters who liked doing coincidence bets. A man whose wife or girl friend is called Anne will do a tenpenny Yankee on horses with Anne in their name - say Boozy Annie, Anniegetyourgun, Princess Anne, Queen Anne - regardless of their chances of winning. Daft, but fun, and why not for a couple of quid stake?

With Williams it was horses named Harry. He did not back anything else, only Harrys. Vic instructed one of his staff to monitor his betting, and the pattern was that he did not back every Harry horse but whenever he did it won.

Sheer coincidence! "No, this fellow's no threat," said Vic.

Well, even the canny Vic Rolls can get it wrong. This time it was to be Mr Williams who was to need a van to carry his winnings to the bank.

For the moment however Mr Williams was just practising, winning little bets on 'Harrys'. Still no alarm bells, but very interesting! He was giving the office a buzz! Rolls laid off his bets in £50 singles, and these about covered their losses.

Then Williams went for the big one.

It was a nice day for it, a bumper Saturday for punters with six meetings to choose from in England and two in Ireland.

And seven horses with Harry in their names.

"He's bound to be on them," said Vic, "Call the other offices and check."

Sure enough, there was an accumulator running reported the Portsmouth shop - an easy drive from Chantry.

True to his style, the intriguing Mr Williams had not backed them all. Two horses with Harry in their names were in early races and he had not backed them, and they did not win. Then, with five left, he laid his bets. He picked all five, laying out a super yankee on his phone account with an ominous £20 accumulator.

The alarm bells rang and soon all hands were on deck monitoring the high street betting shops. Sure enough, several betting shops within half an hour drive of Chantry had taken doubles and patents on the Harry horses. None would land a fortune but in total the winnings would be tasty. And that super Yankee with an accumulator would be a monster!

Other bookmakers also reported lots of small-stake patents and Yankees - and all the Big Three bookmakers all had Harry accumulators going that would each top £1 million.

All eyes were on Harry.

By mid-afternoon three Harrys had won, at Epsom, Sandown and Brighton, but not without drama.

In the Epsom race Harry Karry was running a well-beaten second halfway up the long final half mile but the leading horse suddenly veered sharply left and threw his jockey off.

"Something had seemed to be bothering the horse" a television pundit said when the race was being reviewed. "All the way from the bend it kept swinging its head round as though trying to see where the other horses were!"

While that stewards enquiry was going on Harry's Friend was winning at Sandown but did so only because with three almost in a line 50 yards from the finish, one horse swerved into another, leaving Harry's Friend clear with no chance of being caught.

Over at Brighton Harry Potter won without too much drama, but experienced observers were puzzled by the lack-lustre running of the other three horses in the race. "All the others seemed to be out for an afternoon's chat and stroll," quipped one commentator.

"How many more Harrys are there?" demanded Vic.

"Two, Hopalong Harry at Pontefract and I Love Harry at York."

Hopalong Harry was a no-hoper judged from his past form. He was in a six-runner handicap and was giving his usual dismal performance when all five horses in front of him took the wrong course, despite it being plainly dolled off and all the jockeys making frantic efforts to steer their mounts back on track.

By the time some of them managed to get back into the race, Hopalong Harry had crossed the line at 33-1.

"I don't believe this," joked the commentator, "Hopalong Harry could have hopped all the way and still won!"

"Now for I Love Harry," said Tommy. "If it wins, he will win millions."

"Lay it off," Vic ordered. "He won't get us this time."

Minutes later, after a series of frantic phone calls, Tommy shouted across the office.

"They won't take much, all the big firms have got big accumulators going on the same horse."

"Then everyone will be piling on to the last one in the accumulator just as they did with Frankie's seven at Ascot and it'll be unbackable."

There was a buzz in the office. Everyone was enjoying this.

"What's the roll up so far" asked Vic.

"£28,432.45p, plus another £40,000 in doubles and trebles."

Vic changed his mind. "I Love Harry is forecast at 2-1. No point in laying it off. We have a £500,000 limit and we will be liable for a hundred grand but the big firms will be hammered."

As it happened, there was no need to send money to the course. The news had got around and everyone was piling into I Love Harry, remembering Frankie Dettori's Magnificent Seven just as Vic had forecast.

The betting on I Love Harry opened at 30-100 and that plunged to 1-10 and then 1-20. Many bookies had wiped it off their boards and some were offering the 2nd favourite without I Love Harry.

Vic and Tommy watched the screen as the horses started to line up for the race. "Well, that's it," said Vic. "But whatever happens, from us and the big firms the fellow stands to make a packet."

"Good luck to him," said Tommy. "But it's not over yet - the horse could lose."

"It won't," retorted Vic. "You can bet on it!" They all laughed. They were enjoying this. Williams had given them a bit of excitement.

Anyway, if I Love Harry won, the papers would be full of it, and for weeks everyone would be doing coincidence roll-ups. They would soon get their money back.

Suddenly the television commentator's voice rose with excitement.

"There's something happening down at the start. The handlers are having trouble with one of the horses. I can't see which - yes, I can now. It's I Love Harry. The jockey has dismounted and is leading the horse around, trying to settle him."

"I don't believe this," said Vic. "If the horse doesn't run, he can't lose. I bet he's praying it's pulled out. If it runs at those odds it won't make much more for him."

Then the commentator suddenly shouted with surprise.

"This is extraordinary. The horse has simply flopped down and is refusing to get up. He thinks he is in his field at home and it's time for an afternoon nap!"

There were a few more minutes of this drama then the commentator said: "Yes, as we expected, they are going without him. I Love Harry is still lying down, and no one is going to make him change his mind. The starter has lost patience."

The other runners had been in the stalls some time and were getting restless so without further delay the starter shouted to the jockeys he was going to send them off. Vic flopped back in his chair.

"Well, that's that. He's pulled it off in a way he can't have expected but it will have made little difference to his winnings, not at that price."

"Vic!"

Mike, one of Vic's staff was holding a telephone to his ear, and motioning Vic over.

"What?"

"That accumulator bet, the Portsmouth office says that now all the money is going on to another horse."

"What horse, what race?"

Listening closely to the caller Mike relayed what he was saying to Vic: "His bet stipulated if absent, all on Jack's Lad."

"Jack's Lad? That's running in the same race as I love Harry!"

From the television screen came the crack of the gates opening.

"They're off!" shouted the commentator but Vic was not listening to his commentary.

"What's the odds on Jack's Lad!"

"It's too late to lay anything off now."

"What are the odds!"

"100-1."

Vic laughed. "100-1? No chance!"

He should have kept quiet. It was only a six-furlong race and the words were hardly out of his mouth before the commentator's voice was once again rising towards high C.

"Oh, there's going to be a big upset here. Jack's Lad has sprinted miles clear, the other runners are going to have to hitch a lift on a prayer to catch him. He's going further, four, five, eight lengths. It's all over, and Jack's Lad does not break sweat. His jockey looks round for non-existent dangers and is able to ease him down and crosses the line a good eight lengths clear of the pursuing bunch who all look plodders by comparison. 100-1! There won't be many on that."

"How did he do it?" Vic demanded.

"Luck."

"Luck? That's not luck - that's..." But Vic could not think what it was, but luck? "You don't get luck like that. A hundred to one!"

"There will be a massive rule four," Tommy commiserated.

Because of the heavily odds-on price of I Love Harry there was a 75p in the pound deduction from winning bets.

"Academic!" said Vic. "That's still 25-1, the blighter's whacked us! Twenty-five to one, that's more than enough to hit our limit."

The racing pages were full of the story of the punter who had cleaned up over £5 million with a series of doubles and trebles and five-horse accumulators with all the big firms, all on horses named Harry and the final one called Jack's Lad.

One racing reporter had come up with a fascinating fact. He was a breeding expert, and checking the pedigrees of the horses had discovered that they were all sired by King Harry - hence the 'Harry' in their names, even though they were now owned by five different people, and Jack's Lad, too, was in the same blood line. Jack's Lad was originally meant to be registered as Harry Jack, but the name had been taken so they settled for Jack's Lad.

"It was a whole bloody family!" said Vic.

"That's not all of it!" exclaimed Tommy, after doing some checking of his own. "What nobody noticed is that all the horses are trained in yards in or around Chantry."

Vic took this in slowly, and what he was thinking he did not reveal; it would have been greeted with a horse laugh from the office. But he was thinking: if all the horses were trained near Chantry, they would meet on the gallops around the town.

The story was big news and not only on the racing pages. The punter was not allowing his name to be published, but something was definitely weird and Vic was intrigued. He made up his mind. He was going to meet this Mr John Williams.

The next day being Sunday he left the office in the hands of Tommy and headed for Chantry with a £500,000 cheque for Mr Williams.

Charlie Moon's yard was quiet as the morning exercise work had finished but Vic saw a young stable lass brushing down a horse.

Vic greeted her. "Good morning. I'm looking for Mr Williams."

"Williams?" In a yard full of first names and nicknames she had to think for a moment. "Oh, you might have missed him, he's leaving today

- oh, no, here he is."

Crossing the yard was a man leading a horse.

"Mr Williams?" Vic extended a hand affably.

"That's me."

"I'm Vic Rolls. I've got a nice little cheque for you." Handing him the envelope with the cheque inside Vic added: "Your winnings. Congratulations."

"Ah," Williams responded, surprised. "Thanks. Personal delivery!"

"It's not every day we hand out big cheques like this. I thought personal delivery was called for. Not that you really need this little cheque, I understand you've done the big firms for a bundle. How did you manage it?"

This evoked only an enigmatic smile from Williams.

"You're leaving I hear. What will you be doing with all your winnings?"

"Buying a place in the South of France. Felt like some warmth on my back."

"No more early mornings mucking out, eh?"

"That's right."

"Well, will we be expecting more big roll-ups from you Mr Williams? If so, next time we'll duck!"

Williams shook his head and grinned. It was a very self satisfied grin.

"No, that's enough."

That seemed to be about as much as he wanted to say and with a nod made to continue on his way. The stable lass left the horse she was grooming and went over to the horse Williams was leading and gave it a pat.

"'Bye Harry, enjoy your retirement in the sun, you lucky fellow!"

Williams raised a hand in farewell and walked on, leading the horse to a waiting horsebox.

Turning to the girl Vic queried: "Harry? The horse is called Harry?"

"Yes, a sweet old thing. Well bred, but never made it as a racehorse, too slow, but he was Jack's favourite in the yard. Dotes on him. He spent more time with Harry than he did with us! Talked to Harry like he was human."

A stable lad nearby heard her and laughed.

"Talked to Harry all day. I reckon Jack can talk horse language!"

The girl added: "Harry followed him around everywhere. Always went with him to the races, as a companion to the racehorses."

"He'll miss the horse now he's leaving won't he?"

The girl shook her head. "No. Jack bought old Harry off Mr Moon with his winnings and is taking him with him to the South of France."

"Jack? I thought Mr Williams' name was John."

"No, Jack. Yes, I think it is really John, but Johns get called Jack, don't they?"

The stable lad poked his head round the backside of the horse he was grooming : "There's nothing you can tell Jack about breeding and form. I reckon Jack was a horse in a previous life. He can neigh like a horse. It's his party trick, and if you didn't know, you'd think it was a horse!"

Vic looked down the lane where Williams was preparing to load the horse into a horsebox. Vic knew that he must have heard what the lass and lad had said and there seemed to be a look on his face like 'well, what do you make of that?'

Then Williams patted Harry's nose and said something into the horse's ear and it looked round at Vic, and showed its teeth for all the world like a grin. As Vic turned to get into his car there was a loud neigh - from the horse or Jack? Whoever it came from, to Vic's imagination, which was by now working overtime, it sounded like mocking laughter.

On the drive back to the office Vic could not get that strange little scene out of his head or what the stable lass had said. Harry the horse always went with Jack to the races and the two talked to each other - oh, come on Vic, you don't think the blinking horse was fixing races! Talk about straight from the horse's mouth!

But, if you had a horse you could talk to, and who could arrange with his equine mates who was going to win, and who was to sit down and refuse to race....?

Vic nearly swerved off the road laughing.

No, the fellow was just a lucky punter with a horse he talked to called Harry.

Wasn't he?

Assassin by Post

It took him two months to prepare his murder machine. He spent the time in pubs in London's East End. Drinking, not much, and listening, a lot

Then he had his list. It was long. There are a lot of villains in London. He struck lucky with the first name on it.

Mac Hopper had been noticed as he entered the pub after the killing. Over the next few nights he listened to comments about Hopper from the drink-oiled regulars. It was whenever someone named Biggsy was mentioned in low voices. It had been in the newspapers recently: Biggsy was the name of the dead man found floating in the canal. He got into casual conversation with Hopper over a drink. Yes, there was something about him; evil, soulless. He had underlined Hopper's name and put him top of the list.

A week later he sent the letter.

Hopper got the letter on a Saturday morning. A strange coincidence, as he was reading in his local paper about the ongoing investigation into Biggsy's murder. Hopper - Mac was his nickname, earned because of his reputation with a knife - had topped the mad bastard. These jobs were normally routine; he did them, picked up the money then went down the pub. But the contract from Ric Prezzo was special because Hopper had hated Biggsy since the bastard had been dealer the night Fritzy had taken three grand off him in one hand at poker.

It had been at Harry's Place. Fritzy's fourth queen had come off the bottom of the pack, certain. Mac did not blame Fritzy, it was Biggsy shafting him just for spite. He knew it, in his gut, he knew. Just to get even for the time Biggsy had held a pair of jacks, with a jack, a pair of kings, a six and a five showing on the table and three grand in the pot. Mac had frightened him off with a two grand raise, bluffing that he held a pair of kings. Biggsy folded and then Hopper had laughed and revealed his hand - nothing, ten high.

Biggsy, the big fart, had stormed out.

He had no idea why he was doing Biggsy. That was Prezzo's business. It was a job. Biggsy always walked home alongside the canal and Hopper had just stepped out of the alley, said: "Hello" in a nice friendly way, drove the knife in like the expert he was, and tipped the bastard over the canal wall as he crumpled. The knife followed - he never kept one after a job. Five minutes, five grand.

"Your three grand and raise you two!" Grinning at his joke, Hopper walked back to the pub for a pint.

Recalling all this, he was in the right frame of mind for the letter.

He opened it. More junk mail?

The letter began: 'Mr Hopper.'

Not 'Dear Sir', not 'Dear Mr Hopper'

Then he read the first line.

'You kill people.'

As a way of getting attention, it could not be bettered.

The next line got straight down to business.

'This makes you just the man I need'.

It took him a moment or two to drag his eyes off these sentences and read on.

'I want you to kill someone. If you will carry out this assignment I will pay you £10,000, sent in cash in this manner. To contact me and agree to do this simply put in The Times personal column this message: LubblyJubblyTenGrand.

'I will then send you £1,000 in cash to show good faith and the name of the person.

'Once the job is done - I will read of it in the papers - I will send the final £9,000.

'I know you are the right man for the job. I will not cheat you. There will be other contracts.

'Don't talk about this to anyone, it will only attract unwelcome attention from the police, and you lead a life that is better not looked into too closely. Don't keep this letter and pay for The Times advert in cash. If you are not interested, nothing more will happen'.

Hopper made himself a cup of tea and read and re-read the letter while he drank it.

A nutter? Somehow, he did not think so. Intriguing, very intriguing.

It was a puzzle and he wanted to solve it.

Would this nutter really send him £1,000?

What was he letting himself in for? Hopper never worried about danger; that was what made him successful in the underworld. Hell, he wanted to find out. The price of a small ad, that's all it took.

He went to The Times office and paid for the advert in cash.

The £1,000 in cash and the name of the first victim arrived three days later: Rats Ratten.

Hopper knew of him. A hard case. No problem - not for £10,000, and it wasn't. Another body in the canal.

And the other £9,000 duly arrived.

Only when it did, did it hit him how crazy he had been to do it. Sort of hypnotized by the money and the mystery. But now he was convinced. And had no hesitation when a second offer came: Masher Grant. Easy, Masher, who was usually drunk.

Things were looking good. As well as the money that duly arrived, Hopper had a winning streak at the dogs. Then he got the chance to buy his council flat, special rate as a tenant, and now had the money. Time to put down roots. He was getting middle - aged. Yeah, life was good.

But lucky streaks have a habit of coming to an end.

This time it was when they arrested three well known villains Madman McGraw, Smiler Smith and Toppem Turner. The police were questioning them over the killing and rape of Amanda Appleby, a story that had stayed in the headlines for days six months before.

Hopper knew that Ratten, Smith, McGraw, Grant and Turner often worked together on jobs. Then on the very morning he was reading this, came the third job he had agreed to do for the mystery death-by-post man - and it was McGraw.

Too late now he had been arrested. It did not take much working out. Somebody wanted revenge and had hired him to carry it out.

And that somebody was?

The murdered woman's husband. Who else?

You can bet the others would have been next, after McGraw, except that now it was too late. Damn! That was Hopper's reaction. He had earned £20,000 and now he knew he had been robbed of another £30,000, because no way now would he get the job of doing them. He was right, the evening news carried the story that all three had been charged with the crime.

Because he was a criminal, born and bred, Hopper immediately started thinking about what he could make out this. He had been due 50 grand, and wanted it all.

The answer was simple. Time to make a deal with the husband. Deal? Let's not mince words: blackmail.

No risk. The husband was never going to tell police he had hired him via the adverts to kill them, not unless he did not care what happened to himself, which was hardly likely. He had two dead and three in custody. He would be satisfied with that as revenge enough. He could brazen it out, but he would not welcome an anonymous tip-off to the cops. Now he would want to get on with his life.

Anyway, he could still get someone to deal with the others in prison. Hopper could suggest a few names as part of the deal. Deal? Mincing words again. As part of the blackmail payment.

Hopper was not going to bleed him dry, hell, the man had avenged his wife. But there was more money in this.

Tracking down the husband's address was easy, and one gloomy evening he rang the bell on his front door.

The door opened.

"Yes?"

"Mr Appleby? I'm Hopper. You sent me letters. Can I come in?"

No, he could not. He was kept on the doorstep.

Hopper laid his pitch from there. Just 30 grand, and he would keep his mouth shut.

When he had finished Appleby said: "I don't keep that sort of money in the house."

No bluster. No fear. Eyes of an empty man.

"I'll call back."

"How do I know it will end here?"

"It will. I need the money, but they were bastards. Deserved to die. You avenged your wife. You deserve credit."

It was Hopper being genuine, decent. Yeah, really.

Appleby's expression revealed nothing. "Give me a week."

"OK."

Hopper walked away.

Appleby closed the door.

Det. Inspector Mallory was put in charge of the investigation into the Ratten and Grant killings. Mallory, nearing the end of an illustrious career, had the reputation as one of the Met's top cops, and deservedly so on merit. He was a quiet cop, a thinker; spot-on instinct.

On the interview list was Bookie Norton. Like Ratten, Norton was well known in the lowest circles. They had been enemies. The two had been contesting the Pig Lane territory for years.

"I'm investigating the killings of Rats Ratten and Masher Grant."

"Yeah? What's it to do with me."

"You were not exactly friends."

"You lot should know all about Ratten, you had him in for questioning over that woman's murder. And Grant. They did it, everybody knows."

The Inspector ended the interview. He knew nothing. Thick as two bricks piled end to end.

But he had given him a lead.

The killings could be linked to the woman's murder. The Inspector returned to his office and ordered the file on the burglary killing, and the list of the last six month's murders.

On the list of the dead were two of the burglary suspects.

He picked up the phone. "Sergeant - get the address of Appleby, the husband of woman killed in the Grant Terrace robbery, February this year. Then get round here with a car."

Seeing them Appleby asked: "Have you found out anything?" He did not sound as though he cared much, which was odd.

The police don't answer questions, they ask them.

"You may have read in the papers Mr Appleby.about the deaths of two of the men suspected of your wife's murder."

There was nothing in his eyes. No surprise. Nothing.

"You never read of it anywhere? I see you read a lot of newspapers." The Inspector pointed to a pile of newspapers on the table.

Appleby answered with just one word. "Crosswords."

Mallory noted that the newspapers were all The Times, a paper for crossword addicts.

Then after a moment's silence. "Well, what now? Is that the end of the investigation?"

"We have no more suspects."

"Poetic justice, then."

"But not lawful." The Inspector made to depart. "If anything comes to mind that you think may help, give me a call."

Appleby nodded.

The Inspector felt it was all wrong. He could not fathom why. Something.

He did not have much time to crack it. Six months to go, and retirement.

So Hopper was not the only person to be suspicious of the husband. Mallory could not see anyone else being responsible. He took all the details and sifted them through his mind, and everything went through the sieve except the husband. The victims were prime suspects for his wife's murder. But not a shred of evidence. How could he have done it? His alibis were solid, unbreakable.

Instinct convinces you, but evidence is needed to convince a court. It was Appleby. Somehow it was the husband. He quizzed East End landlords and showed them a photograph of the husband.

Seen him? Two thought maybe... not sure ... maybe.

Then one was sure, well, fairly sure. Yeah, he used to sit in the corner by himself, quiet like.

Strange thing for him to do. He had told police before he was knocked unconscious in the burglary raid he had half-seen one of the attackers when his hood was dragged off. Maybe he thought he would find him. Exact revenge? But he did not, not if his alibis were watertight, and they were.

He sat just by himself?

Yeah, mostly.

Mostly? Anyone you remember him talking to, hung around with?

No, just quiet-like - saw him talking to Hopper one evening.

Hopper?

The landlord was not over-anxious to help. Local hard cases were good customers - and bad enemies. He just nodded.

The Inspector understood and said no more.

Hopper. Local villain. Easy to find. On police files. He lived in a council flat. He invited Mallory in.

Hopper was anxious to look open, helpful. He shifted a pile of newspapers off a chair for the Inspector. Offered him a cup of tea.

No thanks. What did he know about the dead men, in particular anyone who had it in for them.

Nothing. Only what I've read tapping the papers. The Times, the Inspector noted. Hopper did not strike him as a Times reader.

Hopper couldn't help. Wished he could. They were good blokes.

The Inspector did not pursue it. The pub landlord had not been too certain.

After a week Hopper went back to Appleby's house. The place was dark, the windows blank. The building was empty.

He knocked on the door of a neighbouring property and asked the owner about the empty house.

It's been sold, he was told.

"That was quick. There was no sign up last week."

"No, it had been sold weeks before, but the owner only moved out a couple of days ago. I was talking to the agent yesterday. The sale had already been completed but he was allowed to stay on to clear out his possessions."

Hopper walked home thinking. Now what?

He found out a week later when a copy of The Times dropped though his letterbox.

In the small ads was the advertisement: LubblyJubblyTenGrand.

The penny dropped with a sickening clunk. Of course, he had more than his name on his list. Now he had tempted another with a grand through the post.

It did not take an Einstein to work out who the victim would be.

The bastard! Well, we'll see. He could take care of himself.

He was feeling less confident of that by the end of the following week, by which time a regular arrival of The Times through his letterbox revealed the advert had been inserted five more times.

Six hitmen out there and he did not know who they were. Six hoping to get £10,000. Maybe they would all just take the grand and not risk it.

Why show him the adverts? Trying to frighten him off? Maybe. Neat, he had to admit. Warning him not to try any funny stuff. If he did for the husband he ran a risk of getting caught. And the hitmen could still have a go at him, not knowing they were not going to get paid.

Neat, very neat.

He could leave the area. But he had just bought his own place! No, sod it, this was his patch. Nobody ran him off.

But it only took one who like him was intrigued and wanted to see it they would get the other £9,000. Any one of whom might just kill him for some old grudge anyway - there were plenty who would, he had no illusions on that score.

And there could be more adverts.

Sod 'em. Yeah this was his patch. Tough bloke, Hopper.

Nevertheless getting a reprieve made him feel better. And making some more easy money - easy for a pro killer - made him feel even better.

The reprieve came when he got another letter saying: 'I've changed my mind. I've called off the others. If you want to do another job, put OkeyDokey in The Times the same way. Better terms. £20,000.

So another trip to The Times advertising department. Then another letter with £1,000 inside and the name of the victim. But this time there was a card with 'Sorted' printed on it. Leave card at scene, he is instructed.

Deal is, you never try to find me. More work as I said, same terms. No more no less. Quit when you like.

Hopper thought about it. If he did nothing, maybe he would go back on the list. So might as well. The man always paid up.

So Okey Dokey it was.

Mallory ran out of time. Retirement arrived and the trail had gone cold. No evidence.

Just instinct.

It bothered him. He handed over the over the case and passed on what he knew, which in hard facts was very little. He took his pension. But he did not forget.

Then the 'Sorted' killings started making the headlines. The victims had been viciously killed and left with a card with 'Sorted' on it. Nothing else, just 'Sorted'. The pattern was soon clear enough: all the victims had committed rape and murder and were just out of prison having finished their sentences. They included all three remaining suspects of the Amanda Appleby murder, all killed while awaiting trial.

The newspapers picked up a line that all the 'Sorted' murders were of killers and rapists who had served lenient sentences, judged against their wicked crimes. Lately there had been a growing public anger at what was perceived an inadequate sentencing for such savage crimes. So the Sorted killer became a public hero.

"Hope they never catch him," was a comment from a television street interview that summed up the public's feelings.

So did Hopper. Easy money. He wondered who the others doing the jobs were. This husband was some weird character.

Retirement, gardening, holidays. Nice, but that last case bugged Mallory. Always reminded of it when reading the newspapers. Always a murder or two in the papers.

Then Peggy. Crime was no longer a job, a bunch of clues, a sad story in the papers. Now it was family. Peggy, dear darling Peggy. Just 18, walking home through streets as safe as any in Britain, well lighted, not even late at night. Peggy, his only granddaughter. Josie had given him two grandsons, and Peggy was precious. Everybody loved her, bright, smiling, a high flyer at university.

They caught the man, a druggie as usual. Eighteen years, which meant he would be out in ten. Now he felt what he read so often in reports of other people's family tragedies. Ten years! What is ten years. The family's prison sentence is for life, life meaning life.

And it went on, life that is. Of a kind.

Hopper had done alright. Now it had come to end, that was obvious. But greed plays the biggest part in many a villain's downfall. Villain, greed, downfall. The oldest scenario in crime.

The money had not arrived for the last Sorted job. He had overstretched himself, got cocky with all that easy money. Had big ideas and had tried some scams big time. Got so he needed the money, and suddenly it stopped. Now there were a few extra-nasty villains breathing down his neck for some debts. Been feeling his age lately and who needs those sort of enemies when you are feeling your age?

Hopper had kept to the order: Don't try to find me. Not now. He used his contacts and found out where the husband had moved to. This time no 'can I come in?' He just went in.

Where's my money.

The husband did not turn a hair. He indicated the squalid flat. The money's ran out.

Hopper stormed out. Parting words: You better find some. I'll be back.

The flowers and tributes for Peggy were overwhelming. Hundreds, mostly from people - friends and acquaintances of Peggy - they did not know well. We cannot thank them all personally, said his daughter. We don't know their addresses.

What will you do?

Oh, put a advert in the local newspaper, thanking them all. So many, and we will never know who some of them are.

Newspaper speculation was that the 'Sorted' killer was the same person, or gang. It struck a chord; a loud chord. The husband was the obvious one in the East End killings. All the dead had been suspects in the rape and murder of his wife.

The man had been empty, dead. The murder of his wife had killed him as well.

Then the druggie who killed Peggy was murdered in jail, with a 'Sorted' note left on his body.

The newspapers are good at helping criminals, this time they helped Mallory. 'Copycat killer', ran one headline, and the story outlined the writer's theory that the killings were similar to the East End murders.

So now someone was doing the same thing? Couldn't be doing them all, certainly not those in prison. Someone was the organiser. Someone who had suffered, like the husband. Some kind of therapy, an outlet for his pent up hate.

Made sense. Some kind of sense anyway. That is if anything pertaining to murder and rape made sense.

Some kind of therapy? Had it helped the husband? Where was he now? The thought coincided with a voice on the radio. The man was reading out one of those pleas from a listener who wanted to get back in touch with an old love. Of course, you could keep in touch with someone via adverts.

But you can't say in an advert kill so and so. But you can by letter - or the internet. No, the internet is risky, a former colleague who was an expert in computer detective work told him. Things can be traced later.

Old fashioned letters can be shredded, burned. By letter. Of course, by letter! Good old fashioned letter. People sometimes reply to box numbers, never knowing who it is they are writing to. The person from the box number replies, still anonymous.

It was the husband. Not himself, of course. He hired a killer. How? An advertisement. The way the family thanked people for the flowers for Peggy's funeral.

Someone sends a letter, the recipient answers by an advert in a newspaper. That was it! That was how the husband fixed up the killings with local villains. Now, it could be the same with the 'Sorted' killings.

Then he recalled The Times newspapers. And it all fell together. Not proof for a court, not after all this time, but that was how it was done.

He went back and got the files from The Times office on the dates of the murders, and there they were, a cluster of personal advertisement, LubblyJubblyTenGrand, and all in the weeks before the murders.

The newspapers in Hopper's house. The Times, weren't they. Yes. And on the table at the husband's house. Pound to a penny those editions had been the ones he had seen when interviewing them.

He got to work. Got all The Times from a fortnight before the day he had interviewed Hopper. In the personal column adverts, again and again: LubbleJubblyTenGrand.

He updated the search to the period of the Sorted killings and found the same message repeated in the personal columns: OkeyDokey.

He tracked down the husband's new address with the help of old colleagues still in the force. He was in for a shock. The first time he had interviewed the man he lived in an upmarket house in West London. £4 million? At least.

The address he arrived at was a dingy flat over a newsagents in East London.

When the husband answered the door he was in for another shock. The man looked at death's door. Same empty eyes, but now set in deep hollows. Dead man walking.

He did not seem surprised to see the Inspector. Probably did not know he was retired.

"Come in."

On the table was scattered copies of The Times. Mallory was not surprised.

What do you want.

For answer the Mallory picked up one of the newspapers. He riffed through to the personal column.

OkeyDokey, he read out.

The dead face almost smiled.

"When the suspects in the murder of your wife were killed, the message LubblyJubblyTenGrand kept appearing in the same paper. Now this is appearing and people are being murdered."

Appleby just looked at him.

Mallory looked around the dingy room. He said nothing, but his expression did.

Then Appleby answered that expression.

The money ran out.

Mallory nodded, guessing what that meant. He got up to leave. Both knew what should be the next move.

One was sad, resigned. The other dead - empty. Do what you like.

Outside in the street Mallory stood in the shadows and debated with his conscience. What good would it do now?

Then the matter was decided for him.

A figure appeared out of the shadows. It was Hopper. Mallory never forgot a villain. Hopper stood for a minute looking up at the flat window. Then he entered the building.

Mallory flicked open his mobile. His name got him through the top right away.

Hopper and the husband together would have only one explanation. As per his instructions the squad cars arrived fast and silent.

Just in time to catch Hopper as he stepped back out on to the street.

But too late to save the husband. Trademark Hopper killing, one thrust of the blade.

On the husband's body was the card: Sorted.

Hopper had thought that a good joke.

But the joke was on him. And the proof that would eventually put Hopper and a dozen other killers hired the same way in jail - a list of the addresses found in the flat to which Appleby had sent the murder offers.

Mallory attended Appleby's funeral and left a wreath. The note said: 'Thank you. Peggy.'

The Midwinter Murders

Gussie Roberts decided that was enough for today and went to the kitchen to make herself a nice cup of tea. This moving house entailed more work than one would think. She had been in the village for six months and still had not unpacked all the boxes of her possessions.

It was ages since she had sat down with her lap top and typed out her daily 500 words of her next murder mystery. It was annoying as although she jotted down her plots in a notebook as ideas came to her, it was not the same as getting it written down right away.

Also a lot of her time had been taken up in getting to know her new neighbours and already she was quite well known in the village –although no one knew she was the famous crime writer Geraldine Brown. Gussie had always preferred to stay anonymous. Otherwise it was all people wanted to talk about.

Joining the WI and the village hall committee plus the church choir had got her a lot of friends right away. So it was not so surprising that she was one of the first to know about the murder.

Lottie Banks phoned her up while she was having her morning cuppa.

"It's Mrs Greenwood," said Lottie. "Oh it's awful, awful!"

"What is? What's awful?"

"She's dead. Murdered!"

"Oh my goodness! Murdered, you say?"

"They found her in her back garden this morning. Battered to death by a garden spade apparently."

"How awful! Do they know who did it?"

"No. That's the fourth murder this year and its only March. That's one more than we had all last year!"

By lunch time all the friends had got together at Liz Creekmore's house to discuss it.

"The police are quite hopeless," declared Lois Garrett. "That's what? Ten, eleven, murders in two years and they have still not found out who is responsible."

"Didn't I read somewhere that all the victims were people living alone?" enquired Gussie.

"Yes," said Lyn Taylor. "Mrs Gabbs who owned your house before you bought it was one of them."

"It's plainly someone who is mad, who selects those who live alone," said Jenny Greggs.

That sent a shiver through the group, most of whom lived alone.

Things soon settled down, as murders were routine in Midwinter. Gussie got on with her writing and her new social life. But murder fascinated her and over the next few weeks as the police plodded on with their investigations she set about learning more about the murders. The police, of course, as was usually the case in Midwinter, were lumbering along hoping to catch someone in the act.

Men, as women know, are generally pretty hopeless, and the police officers investigating the murders were all men. Gussie, however, was working it out Then there was a bit of a scare in the whist club one evening when old Mrs Sandford-Bloom – Sandy to her friends - did not turn up on time. Neither did she answer her phone when they called but all was well when she arrived late, having dozed in front the fire.

"We were worried about you Sandy," said Doris.

"Why, I'm only ten minutes late."

"Well, with all those ....."

Doris stopped as it was not a topic for a nice game of whist.

"Oh," said Sandy, chuckling, "I keep my doors locked and a big walking stick by my bed!" She was a sparky old dear.

Then Gussie surprised them. "You've got nothing to fear," she said. "None of us here need worry."

They all looked at her with questioning expressions.

"I'll tell you later. Let's just get on with the game shall we?" Gussie liked to set it all up with suitable theatricality.

As they all sat down for a cup of tea the next morning she outlined her theory.

"So, why havn't we anything to fear?" asked Doris.

"Well, all of you have families, oh, here is Inspector Green."

The Inspector, along with Sergeant Fuller, were heading the inquiry into the murders and had been invited by Gussie. They clumped into the room.

"Tea or coffee, officers?"

Once they were settled down with their drinks the Inspector said: "I hope this is not a waste of our time Mrs Roberts."

"Well, let's see," said Gussie, giving him a just-you-wait-and-see-you-impatient-little-man smile.

"I have checked out the family details of all those who have been murdered," said Gussie, "and many of them either had no family to leave their house to, or, in two cases, a relative either too old and in a care home or lived in Australia."

"Yes, we knew that," said the Inspector somewhat impatiently. "What significance is it?"

Gussie paused for effect and then said: "All those house sales have been handled by the same estate agent, the agent who handles pretty well all the sales in this village – Mr Gary Cottam of Cottams Estate Agents, owned solely by Mr Cottam.

"That means a great deal of money in selling fees."

There was an audible gasp from the women, while the Inspector and the Sergeant just stared at her.

"Are you seriously suggesting that Cottam killed them all in order to earn the money from the fees of selling their homes?"

"In a word: yes."

"He is an old-established agent and will not be short of money!"

"Ah, that is not so. Mr Cottam, as you probably know – certainly as the village does and frequently enjoys the gossip – has a rather expensive lady friend. Penny Fowler, one time show girl, small-time actress and, as men rather like, with a very nice figure. She also has expensive, very expensive, tastes. Two or three lavish holidays a year and a wardrobe that would make a millionaire husband blink."

After an amazed conversation with the Inspector – and a promise by the whist drive brigade to say nothing - Gussie outlined her plan to catch Cottam.

A house in the village that was let on a short term lease was used in the plot. A retired woman detective, now of venerable years and looking as likely as anyone to be soon popping her sensible clogs, was installed as the new 'owner'.

After a decent interval she made it known to Cottam that she wanted him to sell the house for her.

"I have no one to leave it to," she remarked, as she explained she intended to use the money for a world cruise and then move to a flat in London.

Thus Cottam was nicely set up.

Then after making and signing the arrangements in writing she phoned him to say she had changed her mind.

Then she waited for the rather annoyed Cottam to murder her before she could cancel her written agreement. A burly copper hid in the spare bedroom ready to foil his dastardly intention.

Cottam's arrest as he broke into house armed with a knife that he plunged into a life-size model of an elderly woman made a nice scoop for the local reporter. He had already made a small fortune from selling stories about the village murders to the national Press.

"So we can now all sleep safely in our beds at night, thanks to Gussie," declared Mrs Grettle and everyone in the whist club clapped.

Unfortunately, this was Midwinter.

There were a few months without a murder but just as everyone was beginning to sleep at night they started up again.

This time the victims were an assorted bunch. Elderly, middle-aged, wealthy (as were most Midwinterians). So the familiar plod plod of the local constabulary started up again.

"Who do you think is doing them Gussie," asked Lottie at their regular coffee morning.

Naturally all the whist club members now looked to Gussie for a solution after her success with the estate agent murders.

"I'm not sure," said Gussie musingly. "There seems to be no pattern."

"Well, if you are puzzled, the police will not have a clue," declared Lottie.

It would have remained a mystery except that Gussie attended a book publishers fair. Chatting to Arthur Swingdeal, an agent who would love to get her on his client list, Gussie happen to mention that she had moved to Midwinter.

This was overheard by another writer.

"Oh, that is the village where Marion Buckler - writes under the name Mandy Murray - lives," he said. "I expect you and her have much to chat about, plotting murders!" He chuckled and moved on.

Mandy Murray - Marion Buckler - well I never, thought Gussie. She had never met or seen a picture of the prolific writer of murder mysteries and she had no idea she lived in the village.

She had read most of Murray's novels, and found them enviably good. And also intriguing. She had a couple of them on her bookshelf and during the next few evenings she made herself a cup of tea and re-read them. It started to dawn on her that the plots reflected the unsolved

Midwinter murders that Gussie knew about.

In particular she noticed that the latest novel by Murray was a carbon copy of the murder two years ago in Midwinter of Lord Bellows, who, for his lordly manner over the villagers over their use of his woodland in which to exercise their dogs, had not been popular.

It had happened three murders previously and when Murray's latest novel, Murder at the Mansion, came out Gussie bought it and stayed up late reading it. It was three am when she had finished it and knew she had solved another murder. The plot was almost a factual report of the murder, following His Lordship's, of Garth Polter, who owned Midwinter's listed mansion Woodhallows.

Polter had been the chief executive of Grand Bank that had been the centre of yet another bank mismanagement scandal that had wrecked so many savings accounts. Not a popular chap, and had not been much mourned by the villagers, several of whom had lost money because of his actions.

Then she looked up the old newspaper accounts of the murders over the past ten years. Apart from the estate agent's murders, the profile of all the unsolved murders exactly fitted the murders in Murray's books.

Gussie set about putting her theory together to present to Inspector Green. But Midwinter is a hive of gossip, and not much stays a secret for long. Buckler was in the Post Office when she overheard Lois and Sandy nattering about Gussie and the way she solved the Cottam murders.

"I saw she has piles of that author Mandy Murray's murder books on her sideboard," said Lois. "Perhaps she is planning to be a crime writer!" Chuckling they left the Post Office.

That was enough for Buckler, whose febrile brain worked it out in an instant.

Gussie had solved the murders. She might assume it was someone who read her books and then copied the murders. But if Gussie found out she was Mandy Murray – which was likely - she would realise it must be her who did them, and the police would soon prove it. There was only one safe course of action. So one more murder had to be planned.

That of Gussie.

But luck was on the side of Gussie, and that was because this was Midwinter. And not everyone in Midwinter was pleased that the murders were finished, because when you have losers you have winners. And the murders had made Midwinter famous.

George Kent had for the past ten years made a very tidy income from his bus tours of Midwinter. Every week he took a busload of sightseers – usually ghoulish old folk – on a tour pointing out the murder spots.

"On the right, Thorn Cottage, where two bodies were dug up in the potato patch three years ago."

"Now we are passing Meadow Barn, where Lady Penelope was strangled by her lover who himself was shot by the postmistress he had jilted."

"On our left the cottage where Butcher Bell who carried out the mincemeat murders lived."

And so on. £1,000 a week pure profit after expenses.

But thanks to Gussie the supply of murders had dried up, and fewer old ghouls booked his tours. Bad enough, but he too was infatuated with the expensive Penny Fowler, and like Cottam, had lost his money along with his brains for her favours.

His bitterness had been stoking up for weeks and finally he decided to murder Gussie.

Not a chap for clever plots, Kent just got himself a big iron bar and waited for a dark moonless night. Then, his resolve bolstered with a few whiskies, he crept through the dark lanes of Midwinter – it was full of such lanes, all tailor-made for a murderer – he made his way to Gussie's cottage.

Fortunately it was just the right dark night for Buckler to carry out her plan, which she had to enact in a hurry before Gussie contacted the police. So armed with an axe she had set out to silence Gussie. She crept round the back of the house and levered open the back door – her previous murders made her a very cool and efficient housebreaker.

Luckily for Gussie at that moment she felt a rather urgent need to visit the bathroom – probably that rather doubtful curry she had with her coffee club friends – and when Buckler entered the kitchen through the back garden, she found the drawing room empty.

When Kent got to the cottage a few minutes later he was somewhat too inebriated to be surprised to find Gussie's back door open at that time of night.

Buckler was carefully feeling her way around in the dark when she heard Kent. Thinking it was Gussie investigating she dealt his dark outline a mighty wham on the head. He fell flat and as she bent over him to finish the job, he managed to roll away, get up and give her an even mightier wham in return that finished her off in one go.

Then he collapsed and died alongside her.

Gussie enjoyed a good night's sleep as she did not go downstairs until the morning and found the bodies. When they had been taken away she gave all her notes on Buckler's - Marion Murray's – murders to the Inspector and went off to meet her friends for coffee.

In Midwinter life goes on.

Gussie was quite happy that the police took the credit for solving all the murders and was able to get on with her writing incognito. She and her friends settled back into their nice routine of coffee mornings and whist drives.

But for how long?

After all this was Midwinter.

Lost in a Dream

It was a dream that had occurred regularly of late. His dreams were becoming more vivid lately. Dreams always fade with the awakening dawn and are forgotten by the time breakfast is eaten. This dream would no doubt have faded in the light of morning and been soon forgotten, but it occurred so vividly and frequently it became established in his memory. So he took to trying to analyse it.

The setting of the dream was various, but the theme was always the same. He was in a situation where he was lost and indecisive about what to do and sought directions and help from people. At first they always said of course they would help, and he would feel relieved and waited for them to do so. But somehow they never did, were always vague in their directions, procrastinating, and he never got to where he wanted to go. Then in the dream he realised that he never really knew, or somehow forgot, where it was he had wanted to go. All he knew was that it was important. There was never any fear or panic, but always a growing frustration; a sense that no one would help.

At work and in his leisure time he was always positive, and did and achieved what he wanted, but never in the half-world of his dreams. It was strange but not alarming. Frustrating, annoying, puzzling.

Sometimes during the day a faint remembrance of the latest dream would flit through his mind. It would make him consciously assert himself, and be positive in what he was doing at that moment. He did not like the indecisiveness of his dreams entering his real life. Those was the only times the dreams bothered him.

It during one of those moments when he was thinking about the dreams and the feeling of helplessness they brought on that made up his mind to assert himself. So he booked an appointment to see a psychiatrist.

Sat in front of the psychiatrist he felt foolish. Hesitantly, self consciously at first, he tried to explain.

"It's curious dream. It is repeated in many guises but I have come to realise that it has a central theme - one I cannot understand.

"The theme is always the same. I am in a situation when something goes wrong, and I need other people to help me. I can't remember every situation I have dreamt but the theme is always very similar. For example, one that recurs is I set out for a new place and when I get there I have to make sure I get the last bus or train back. But I have run out of money.

"For some reason I cannot telephone anyone I know to come and fetch me. I am asking people to help, and at first everyone is bright and helpful and say 'in a minute' or 'come with me'. I wait and follow and then they start to become vague in their response.

"I ask someone else and the same sequence occurs - they know I want help but they do nothing. They are not hostile or unkind, just vague and unresponsive after first agreeing to help. In last night's dream I was fifty miles from home and it was getting dark. I had no money. It was strangely frustration - not frightening or sinister, just helpless, everything in abeyance. An inability to determine events. Then it ended and I woke up.

"I remember another dream a long time ago when I was moving from one room to another in a kind of spiral journey, each room getting smaller and the spiral getting tighter and going nowhere. No fear, nothing; just no purpose, no escape.

"In another recurring dream I am climbing a narrow stairway. It gets narrower and narrower and starts to become a circular stairway. Eventually I am curled tight up in a narrow space, and then the dream ends."

He stopped, and grinned self-consciously, wishing he had not explained the silly dreams to this stranger, but at the same time with the comfort that it was to a professional psychiatrist.

"Very interesting," said the psychiatrist.

"What can you do?" said Gordon.

"It's alright. I will help. Just wait. That's enough for today. I will make some notes."

"When will we....?"

"I'll see you next week."

He returned the next week to the psychiatrist. He sat and waited while the psychiatrist studied the papers in front of him.

Eventually he said, "I will help you. Make an appointment for a week's time with my secretary."

That night he dreamt he was in London and had lost his way. He asked people the way, although in the dream he did not know where he wanted to go.

A week later he kept the appointment with the psychiatrist.

"What have you decided?" he asked.

"Nothing yet. It is very interesting case. I will do some research. We'll meet in fortnight."

It was unhelpful, unsatisfying. Just like his dreams.

That was what made him decide to book the holiday. He had been looking in a travel agent's window at a Greek islands cruise holiday when the previous night's dream came back to him. He had been in a town and had got lost. He kept asking people the way to somewhere that in the dream he did not know where. Everyone he asked was vague, and walked on leaving him. Then the dream ended.

He had been thinking of taking a holiday for some time. Lately he had stopped at the travel agents several times thinking about the advert in the window of a Greek Islands cruise.

He had stopped again today to think about the holiday when the feeling of helplessness, of indecision of the dream, came back to him. To blast it away he grabbed hold of himself and went into the travel agents and booked it. It was for a week, and he would be back for the psychiatrist appointment.

The cruise was good. Nothing to decide, everything done for him, no planning or decisions. Just drift along with events.

They called at an island and the passengers were allowed ashore. Three hours, enough time for a leisurely drink by the harbourside and a stroll around. He lost his way in the back streets, and asked the way to the waterfront from man who spoke English.

I'll show you, the man said. I must just do something first. He went into a house, and then came out and walked away, pointing down the road. That way, he said. He walked down the road and it was a dead end. He climbed a small hill and looked seawards and saw the cruise ship leaving the harbour.

From his vantage point on the hill he could see practically all the round the island. The tourist map told him it was two miles long and half a mile wide with a population of just a hundred.

Lying five miles off the coast of Greece the island was without an airfield and the ferry plied only once a week. Switch off your mobile and it was just the place for a getaway from life's pressures. Oddly, missing the ferry did not trouble him. The island seemed a nice place to spend a week. No point in worrying. He breathed in deep of the fragrance of the spring flowers rising from the valley below. He was beginning to unwind already. The perfect choice for a holiday.

Every day he walked right round the island. One day he stood the hill and saw the ferry come in and depart. Somehow he had forgotten it was due. He would have to wait until the next ferry.

He often asked people when the ferry was due. They would tell him; soon, next day. He soon ran out of money. Somehow he had forgotten to bring his credit card.

He found work at the café. How he had started to work there he could not remember. The pay was enough to live on. He started saving for the ferry fare, but he never had enough. He wrote a letter home asking for money to pay his fare back but somehow he never got round to posting it.

One day someone would help him get back. But they never did.

The islanders grew used to seeing him wandering round the island. After a while they stopped wondering who he was.

1918

Their story became part of the village history. It was like a Greek tragedy, or a tale by Shakespeare, as one literary local in the village pub observed.

George and Elizabeth had known each other since their village schooldays. She was the prettiest girl for miles around and he was the village's bit of a lad. Happy, handsome, all the local girls had their eye on him. Every Saturday night at the village dance, the girls vied with each other to catch his eye.

But Elizabeth was the one who everyone expected would catch him and they were proved right when they started walking out. They would get married and settle down just as everyone had always expected. There was no prettier girl in the county. He was a lucky young man, everyone said so.

"When are you two going to name the day," village gossip Mrs Barlow demanded one day when encountering them in the village main street. "Faint heart never won fair lady!" she chided, wagging a playful finger at George.

"Make him buck his ideas up, Elizabeth!"

George grinned bashfully while Elizabeth smiled happily and hung on his arm.

The wedding plans became something of a communal affair, with both families enthusiastically putting in their pennyworth.

But it was 1917 and George was 18, and the war in the Flanders mud interrupted their plans. The war was a great adventure to George and his mates, and they all volunteered enthusiastically. Their last date was in the village pub where everyone assembled to say cheerio to them.

It was a lovely sunny day when they left the village on their great adventure, full of patriotic pride.

A cheering, flag-waving crowd of villagers saw them off at the station. Elizabeth ran along the platform holding George's hand as he leaned out of the carriage window.

He was thinking of her as they waited to go over the top. Those sunny days seemed lovelier and sunnier as the rain poured down. Crouched in the trenches he and his mates waited to see if they were about to die, or live this time to face the same question the next day. He had survived nearly a year, but every day seemed it would be the last.

There was a blinding flash and a mind-crushing explosion. Disoriented, in a strangely different - peaceful - world, he stumbled through the night after losing his way.

After the stink and mud of the trenches and the head-thumping gunfire it was like heaven. He was walking again as a young man - a young lover - through his own village on the Sussex Downs, hand in hand with Elizabeth. Lovely Elizabeth, the girl he was going to marry.

When the dawn broke he had kept going, judging the direction back to his own lines as best he could by the sun shining through the morning mist. The peace in the mist had been beautiful after the noise and slaughter in the trenches. Then the mist had cleared and he found himself on the edge of a village.

He was completely lost. For the first time for months he felt safe.

He was hungry. On the edge of the village was a house set back from the road. Chickens scratched around it and beyond he could see cows grazing. A farm would have food. They might give him some. Then he saw the young woman.

She was engrossed in scattering food for some chickens and did not see him at first. Then she looked up. He held up his hand as a peace gesture. Realizing he was carrying his rifle he laid it on the ground to give her assurance.

He remembered the French he had learned at school.

"Je suis faim." He touched his stomach and enacted drinking. "Merci," he added. It was a bizarre scene and he had to smile. That made her smile too.

"Un moment," she said and went into the house. She returned with a cup of water.

She watched him as he drank. The extraordinary, other-world, peace since leaving the trenches still suffused him.

Suddenly she grasped his arm, and pulled him towards the house.

"L' Allemagnes," she said urgently, pointing along the road.

She ushered him into a back room from where he could hear the German convoy passing. When all was quiet she returned with a plate of food. It was then she saw the dried blood that matted his tunic and had run down his trousers in a red river.

She cleaned up the wound. Then she led him to an attic room overlooking the farmyard. "Restez aqui," she said.

"Merci," he said, "Je suis George."

She smiled and repeated, "George." Her pronunciation made him smile.

She laid a hand against her breast. "Danielle."

He held out his hand but his French ran out. "Glad to know you Danielle."

She shook his hand and attempted his English greeting, which made her laugh.

Every day she tended his wound

Occasionally a German patrol passed by. Even when they did, it did not disturb the deep sense of peace and belonging that filled every day.

He reckoned he could not be more than a few miles from the trenches but it was so peaceful and quiet.

After a couple of weeks he was able to walk without pain. He started to help out on the farm, dressed in clothes the family gave him. He knew it was because of her persuasion her parents allowed him to stay.

He had never felt so certain of what he wanted in life.

By then he was deeply in love with her.

The flu epidemic swept into the village silently and savagely, and Elizabeth was one of the first to fall ill. As she lay in her bed it gave her great hope and comfort thinking of him and re-reading the letters he had sent her. Fearful she might never see him again she wrote a letter telling him how much she loved him, telling her mother to send it only if…

"Don't! Don't talk like that! "her mother scolded, hiding her tears.

. The German patrols started to pass more frequently. Once or twice they called at the farm to buy produce. At those times he hid. But it began to worry him. If they spotted him and started talking he would surely give himself away. If that happened, what would they do? He was putting the girl and her family in danger.

The guilt he had of not returning to his unit now began to trouble him. He was a fool. Here on the farm he was safe. No one would know he had not been killed. How many had gone over the top, never seen again, buried in that bloody mud. But he had to live with himself. He was not a coward.

The sound of guns would guide him back and he would find his unit. He would not be shot for cowardice. He was not a coward: cowards did not return.

He put on his uniform and collected his gun. "Je retour," he said as she clung to him.

"Je t'aime," she pleaded.

"I will come back," he promised. "Je t'aime. I love you."

The last sight of her as he walked away was of her standing at the farm gate, waving. He waved back until he could no longer see her, then turned and headed into the sound of gunfire.

Eventually he made his way back to his unit. Even in the short time he had been gone, very few old comrades were left.

"I was concussed," he told his sergeant. "I lost my way."

It was going to be a long war. Even he survived he was not going back to England. It was hard, cruel, but it was not right not to be honest.

He sat down in the trench and wrote the letter to Elizabeth, telling her he loved another. He did not want her to waste her life waiting for him. Even he survived this war he would stay in France.

He handed the letter in for posting and the next day went over the top in yet another of the mad, wicked, pointless, suicide assaults. He was one of the first to be killed. He fell back into the trench and an explosion immediately buried his body.

His family received the news the day after Elizabeth died, her last letter to him still not posted. His letter to Elizabeth arrived a day after she died.

The grieving families met and decided to bury her with both letters unopened beside her in her coffin.

"They must have died on the same day," said George's mother, as she sat over a cup of tea, commiserating with Elizabeth's mother.

"Together in life; together forever in death," read a wreath provided by both families.

Their story became a village legend: a great love story. A Greek tragedy as the man in the village pub said.

In France Danielle was left to play her part in the legend. Had he been killed? Did he really love her?

She spent her life never knowing.